MY THREE
FAVORITE
NOVELS

MY THREE

FAVORITE NOVELS

AS SHAKESPEARE WOULD HAVE WRITTEN THEM

D. B. CLARK

EDITED BY CAROL CLARK

MY THREE FAVORITE NOVELS
AS SHAKESPEARE WOULD HAVE WRITTEN THEM

iUniverse books may be ordered through booksellers or by contacting:

iUniverse
1663 Liberty Drive
Bloomington, IN 47403
www.iuniverse.com
1-800-Authors (1-800-288-4677)

ISBN: 978-1-5320-9907-6 (sc)
ISBN: 978-1-5320-9908-3 (e)

Print information available on the last page.

iUniverse rev. date: 04/23/2020

CONTENTS

INTRODUCTION

Others have claimed that *Mob Dick* is a great novel, and I certainly believe that Moby Dick belongs on that list. But this is a book about my favorite novels, and I am hoping that my giving them the *as Written By Shakespeare* treatment will add them to your list of favorite novels.

This second of my favorite novels, *The Count of Monte Cristo,* like *Moby Dick*, is filled with the history of the time, the time when Napoleon was exiled on the Isle of Elba, and then escaped to attempt to rule again, only to ultimately be exiled to Saint Helena. Much of the action in The Count of Monte Cristo takes place during the time when the French King XVII ruled.

The Hobbit, of course, is not a great novel, and it is not at all historical, it is a fantasy. But it is one of my favorites, so I hope that my personal version of it will make it one of your favorites too.

Shakespeare didn't write novels, he wrote plays, and his plays were poetry in the form of Iambic pentameter, with lots of dialog and many metaphors. On the other hand, Moby Dick and the Count of Monte Cristo are novels, and these two novels spent a lot of time describing the history their times. Shakespeare's plays plays were often historical, but the action and interaction of his characters was more important to him. I chose, like Shakespeare, to skip most of this history, and stress the action. So, if you like history, read history books.

MOBY DICK

AS TOLD BY SHAKESPEARE

ACT I

SCENE I: THE NARRATOR BEGINS THE PLAY

Playgoers, let me introduce this play
As Herman Mellville introduced his novel
"I am Mellville, but call me Ishmael.
Since I had always longed to sail the seas,
My parents humored and then encouraged me
To follow my dream of becoming a sailor.
So, low and behold, I left Manhattan Island
Intending to board a whaling-vessel
At the port of New Bedford, Massachusetts."

And adventitious Ishmael continues his story.
But no vessel would depart for many a day,
So, I needed to find an inn in which to sleep.
So, I sought the inn where most sailors
Would seek a room, and this turned out to be
The Spouter Inn, and there, the crowded bar room
Was filled with sailors from ever port in the world,
Some looking so weird looking that they would
Frighten soldiers, and one was even a giant of a man
Who was so covered with square tattoos
That I couldn't tell whether he was black or white.
It turned out that his name was Queequeg,
And he was a native the south Pacific isles.
And, low and behold, when I asked the innkeeper
For a room for the night, he said he only one room,
But it had only one bed, and so I would have to sleep
With Queequeg, the tattooed giant.
"No! No!" I insisted I wouldn't sleep
With that primitive giant,
For I remembered him on the streets
Selling shrunken heads,
Almost causing the elegant
New Bedford ladies to faint.

3

But, low and behold, I found myself sleeping
With Qqueegeg, whose long arm
Was draped lovingly across my chest,
An arm that was so heavy I couldn't move it.
But alas, I finally o slipped from beneath
That massive arm. But then Squeegee
Woke with a start, And grabbed his harpoon
And hatchet and thrust them toward me,
I was so frightened; my heart almost stopped beating,
And I knew I was going to die,
But then Queequeg smiled the most
Gentle of smiles, And quietly whispered,
"Sorry, young sir, No, no I will not kill ye,
And we will be shipmates
On our first voyage together sailing to Nantucket.

And so it was that Queequeg, the tattooed,
South Pacific cannibal headhunter from Kokovoku and I
Became cherished shipmates, as we would be
To end of our whaling voyage, I vowed, *as we, set out to sea!*
And low and behold, what a sea it would be!
No, what I saw, when our ship took to sea
Was not a water world but an explosion of birds,
And an acrobatic exhibition of somersaulting dolphins
That was a performance that I knew was only for me.
But how could this be? I was but a simple sailor
And not an aristocrat who deserved such a show.
So, I looked at Queequeg, and described what I saw.
He looked puzzled, and then sighed,
"All things beautiful must die, so live while you can.
That is what I am trying to do, so you should do it too."

So I looked away and wondered if this primitive man
Was really a great philosopher, or perhaps a visionary.
And I wondered what I was going to learn from him
About the ending of our voyage. Was it to be fate
That determined our ultimate destiny? We would see.

4

But enough of this fanciful pondering.
We were merely two simple sailors setting out to sea.
Our destiny was just likely to be a return to port,
With our without our casts full of whale oil,
Of which our share of the profits would probably
Be minuscule And barely enough for us
To purchase a pint of ale at the Spouter Inn.
So much for my silly wondering. I was just setting
Out to sea. to see what this simple and
Gloriously happy young sailor would see.

But who actually was my magnificent and gentle
And beloved shipmate? My friend was not one to brag,
But by gentle prodding, I eventually learned
His amazing history. Queequeg was royalty,
Queequeg was a prince of a South
Pacific island who Decided he wanted
To see the other side of the world,
So he threw himself on the deck of a whaling ship,
And when even the captain's threat to chop off
His clinging hands, didn't make Queequeg
Leave the ship, The captain let him stay to become
The harpooner I knew him to be.

When we arrived at Nantucket,
Queequeg and I found a place to eat and sleep
Called, Try Pots Inn, and since Queequeg,
Before sailing, Needed to do his Fasting and
Humiliation ritual, he asked me to seek out
The best whaling ship. So, I saunter down to the
Nantucket docks and settled on the a battered
Whaler whose name was Pequod.
Trying to look confident, I climbed onto deck,
Where there stood what was obviously
A well worn whaler and asked if he be the Captain.
"By The North Sea, no, I be Captain Peleg,
Owner of this cherished vessel,
And who be you, sir, who has come aboard my ship?

5

"I be," I started, and then changed it to I am, Ishmael."
And then another old sailor joined in,
And I be Bildad, second owner of this good ship, Pequod.
And I gather by your sailor clothes that you wish
To join my crew." "I do indeed, wise
And venerable sir, I wish to be a whaler.
The he eyed me, and shook his head,
"Mighty young you are, boy, but can you hurdle a
Harpoon?" "Eye, wise sir, just like
I hurled sacks of grain at home."
"But did your grain sacks pierce any whales?"
"Nay, wise sir, but I'll buy me a hefty harpoon,
And pierce every wicked whale that I see."
The first old man looked me over slowly,
And the shook his head. "I'll think about it,
I'll think about it, young boy."
Seeing his hesitation, I quickly argued,
"Obviously you see that I am still learning,
But I have best friend and bunk mate
Who is the world's best harpooner,
His name is Queequeg, and he is a giant of a man
Who has sailed from the South Pacific
And killed hundreds of whales every day
Along the way." "Well, this person I would see,
This person I would see." Said Captain Peleg.
Having given my Exaggerated description of my friend
I jumped off the Pequod and dashed back to the
Try Pots Inn, There. I tried to enter our room,
But the door was bolted from the inside.
I shouted, "Queequeg, It's me, Ishmael,
Let me in!" There was no response, so I shouted,
"Queequeg, I've got us to be signed up
On the Pequod, the best ship at Port Nantucket,
Please open the door." There was no response,
So rearing back, rushed the door so hard
That crashed it open, then fell to the floor,
Almost landing on Queequeg,
Who was still squatting on the bunk

In his Fasting and Humiliation position.
And he still didn't move. "Queequeg, wake up,
Wake up! They're waiting for us To sign papers,
I've told them what a great harpooner you are, and they
Want to see you prove it." That stirred him,
And he slowly rose from the bunk,
"Lead on, eager shipmate," he grinned,
I will show them even more than you claimed."
So, we rushed back to the Pequod
And called forth both of owner.
When they saw the giant Queequeg,
They tried not to gasp, and only barely Whispered,
"Yes, yes, please show us, Great sir." Then
Queequeg drew back His great harpoon, and said,
"See ye, The knot on the distant sail post,
Now watch me pierce it, though gentle,
And if it be a giant whale, it would go
Right through its iron hard skin.
Thus Say, Queequeg, gentle tossed
His harpoon. And sure enough, it struck
The very center of the knot.
"Sign on, sign on!," both owners shouted."
And so Queequeg and did so,
And then we hurried back to the
Try Pots for a huge diner, and to
An old sailor chant this old whaling tale:

Oh, ye sweet little girlie
Ye sweet little girlie
Of this old tavern,
Of this old tavern,
See ye the whale,
The great white whale,
The great white whale,
With great white tail,
With great white tail
That wags in the wind,
That wags in the wind,

And then sweet girlie,
Sweet little girlie,
See now my harpoon,
My lethal harpoon,
My lethal harpoon,
Sinks into the flesh,
Sink into the flesh
Of the great wicket whale,
The great wicked whale,
The great wicket whale,
And then, my sweet girlie,
My sweet little girlie,
My sweet little girlie,
See me come home sailing,
See me come home sailing,
To bring to the owners,
To bring to the owners,
My casts of rich oil,
My casts of rich oil,
To set before the owners,
To set before the owners,
Who cast me my small portion,
Cast me my small portion,
So I can purchase your sweet favours,
Can purchase your sweet favours,
My sweet little girlie,
My sweet little girlie,
My sweet little girlie.

And then after marveling at this old sailors creaky,
But still clear voice, we crept up to our room
For a happy night sleep. On the way, however,
I asked Queequeeg if he didn't think that
The old sailor's chantey was a bit naughty
And disrespectful of the tavern maiden.
After all, that's what my Christian upbringing told me.
But Queequeeg merely smiled and responded,
"Maybe the tavern maiden would think otherwise.

Have you ever thought what your girls back home
Would want to feel?" Once again, Queequeg,
The primitive savage was proving to be a philosopher.
And we were ready to board the Pequod the next morning.
But we were surprised and a little worried
That was no actual Captain on the bridge,
Even though the full crew was on board,
And the First Mate, Starbuck was on the bridge.
Queequeg and I could only look at each other,
And wonder, and maybe be just a little bit worried.
That actually Captain was not on the bridge
To greet his new or returning crew.
Then we watched as that crew came aboard.
These whalers were members were like
A well-oiled sports team.
And the team captain was followed
By The next most skilled team members
And on to the least skilled team member.
But then we realized that this was not a boys team
Fighting for glory. This was a team of murderous warriors,
Who would attempt to slaughter another murderous warrior.
To utter destruction of one or the other,
That was at the end of this non-boyhood game.
On this oceanic battlefield, the team leader
We now learned was Captain Ahab. And his
Killing crew was made up of his boat steers,
Or sometimes called his squires,
And his killer harpooner was Parsee.
And then Captain Ahab was followed by his first mate,
Who was Starbuck, and his Harpooner was
Daggo, who was followed by the second mate,
Stubb, whose harpooner was Tashtego,
Who was followed by the third mate, Flask,
Whose Harpooner was Fedallah
And the characters of Pequot's ship leaders were all different.
Captain Ahab's character will be revealed by his later actions.
The slender first mate Starbuck's character was as steady
As his Quaker heritage. He could always be depended on

9

To do what his Christian upbringing told him he must do.
The second mate, Stubb, was an easygoing fun maker,
Who always tried to make the shipmates laugh,
And he was usually very successful.
And his harpooner was Daggo
The third mate was pugnacious Flask,
Who seemed to believe that whales were his
Personal affront, And he intended to punish that disrespect.
Flask's harpooner was Fedallah, who was a six-foot-six
African giant who was as a tall an African giraffe.
Ahab finally there emerged from his cabin
Captain Ahab, muttering, "It feels like coming up
From one's tomb." And now Ishmael realized
That the Captain was indulging in what seemed to be a ritual.
He came on the bridge and walked back
And forth on the planks, muttering to himself things Ishmael
Couldn't quite make out. Then, the second mate Stubb
Followed, saying to himself, "That if Captain
Ahab was please to walk the planks,
Then no one could say nay, that is his rightful way.
Then, after further muttering, the Captain said,
"I am a cannon-ball, Starbuck, and thou wouldst
Wad me down me that fashion?
But I forgot, Stubb, go below to thy nightly grave
Where such as ye sleep beneath shrouds
To use yet the filling of one last dog, and kennel!"
Starbuck was speechless a moment, then said excitedly,
"I am not used to be spoken that way, Sir,
I do but less than half like it, sir."
"Avast!" Ahab gritted between his set teeth,
And violently moving away as if he was
Trying to avoid some passionate temptation.
"Not yet, sir," said Stubb, emboldened,
"I will not tamely being called a dog, Sir"
And then the Captain barked "Then be called
Ten times a donkey, or a mule, and an ass,
Or I'll clear the world of thee!
At this, Ahab advanced upon Stubb

With such overbearing terrors in his aspect
That Stubb involuntarily retreated, saying,
"I was never served so without giving a hard blow for it."
But then Stubb descended to his cabin, wondering,
"Should I go back up, or should
I kneel down and pray for him."

I, Ishmael, was both puzzled by and a little frightened
By Stubb's anger at and resistance to his Captain.
The puzzlement was understandable, Ishmael was new
To whaling. But he was mostly frightened.
The Captain, upon whom he was most dependent,
Seem out of control, perhaps even insane.
It was as though he was an ice-hard man was could melt
With the heat of his anger. And if the man upon whom
All on the ship could melt, then the ship
And all its crew would sink down into
The bottom of the sea? And what was there, darkness?
Or even worse, some great white monstrous
Whale? Then suddenly, Ishmael felt he was having
A vision. At the end of his first whaling voyage,
That he had been so eagerly awaiting,
And even romantically anticipating,
Was all whaler's greatest fear to be realized
Some monstrously murderous white whale
Waiting to massacre all whalers.

But then I, Ishmael, pulled myself
Back from this brink of Hell.
Thank Heavens, I remember the way my shipmates
Had pulled themselves back from that same perdition—
That unholy ritual, that pulling together
Of all the shipmate's unbelievable
And unobtainable strengths.
Captain Ahab was the Satanic-seeming
Symphony orchestra, and he call the string
Instrument leaders To direct the percussionists
To set the beat, and this was done by all

Of the shipmates banging anything metal together,
Or just stamping their feet. The orchestra
Leader, lead or more like raved,
For the most formidable of orchestra members,
The three harpooners, Parsee, Tashtego, and xxx
Who seem totally bewildered by what was happening,
Has, nevertheless, begun clamoring louder than anyone else.
And I, Ishmael, was thoroughly captured by this chaos,
And I joined in happily, and all my bottom of the ocean fears
Gentlly flooded out of even the depth of my Christian soul.

Now, Captain Ahab seemed to have used his orchestral ritual
To almost become a functional captain of a workable whaler.
From his captains cloak, he retrieved a gold coin,
Which he nailed to the mainmast, shouting, "Look ye,
Whoever ye raises me a white-headed whale
With a wrinkle brow and a crooked jaw,
And three holes punctured in his starboard fluke,
Shall have gold ounce, my boys!" "Huzza! huzza!
Cried the eager sailors. "Huzza! huzza!"

The Captain Ahab took charge again, "Advance ye mates,
Cross your lances full before me. Well done!
Let me touch the axis." So saying, with extended arms,
He grasped the three level, radiating lances
At their crossed center. And then directed his intense
G gaze at Starbuck, Studd, and Flask,
But they all looked away, and then Captain
Ahab cried, "In vain, but tis well. Down lances.
And now, ye mate, I do appoint three cup bearers
To my three pagan kinsmen there,
My three most honorable gentlemen and noblemen,
My valiant harpooners, disdain the task?
Cut your seizings and draw the poles, ye harpooners!"
Silently obeying orders, the three harpooners now stood
With the detached iron part of their harpooners,
Some three feet long, held barbs up, before him.
"Stab me not with that keen steel! Cast them over!

Know ye not the goblet end? Turn up the socket!
So, so, now ye cup-bearers, advance. The irons! Take them;
Hold the while I fill!" Forthwith,
Slowly going from one officer
To the other, he brimmed the harpoon socket
With the fiery water from the pewter.
"Now drink, and swear ye men,
That the dreadful whaleboat vow, *Death to Moby Dick!*
And then with his free hand, he waved them to disperse,
Which they did, as Ahab retired within his cabin.

But the absence of Captain Ahab had not left me unaffected.
As I learned of his history with the white whale monster,
Ahab's quenchless quest became mine,
And it also haunted my sleep.
It was from that restless sleep
I was awaken by his demanding,
"Did you hear that voice?" Ahab asked.
"It sounded like a cough." "Careful with
That bucket you're hauling, you'll wet
Our already soggy biscuits!" "No, hear me,
I got sharp ears!" "Grin all you like,
There is someone down in the after-hold
That's not been seen on deck. I suspect that our old Mogul
Knows something of it too. I heard Stubb tell Flask
On morning watch that there's something
Of that sort in the wind." "Hey, watch the bucket!"
And that was definitely the last of my sleep.

As we gazed over the lead colored water, Queequeg and I
Were carefully weaving a sword-mat for an additional
Lashing to our boat when someone's voice
Was starting to sound so strange, like a long drown,
Musically wind so unearthly, that I dropped the sword-mat.
Then, high above in the cross-trees was Tashtego bellowing,
"There she blows! There she blows!" "Where away?"
Was the response. "On the lee-beam, about two miles off,
A school of about twenty." Instantly, all was commotion.

The sperm whale blows as a clock ticks with the same
Reliable uniformity. "There goes flukes!" was now the cry
From Tashtego, And the whale disappeared.
"Quick eastward!" cried Ahab. "Time! Time!"
Then Tashtego Reported that the whale
Had gone down toward the lee-ward,
Then looked again, apparently expecting to
Report that the flukes Were directly in advance of our
bow. But then there was a sudden exclamation from
Tashtego that took eyes From the whale to
Ahab, who was surrounded By five dusky
Phantoms that seemed freshly formed
Out of the air. I could make nothing
Of these dusky phantoms, so I tried to shove them
Aside, and that wasn't too hard.
The whaling adventure that I had so longed for
Had began to happen. After nights sinking
Into the Hell of his cabin, Captain Ahab became
The whaling captain I had expected.
He come on deck early and immediately took charge.
Barking commands that everybody, *except me*,
Seemed to understand, and the long experienced crew,
Did exactly as the captain demanded,
Although I at least did my best not to get in the way.
And to my surprise, I mostly succeeded.
And more important, I was learning.
In a day or so, the call rang out,
"Whale away!" "Where to," the Captain demanded.
"To lee-south," was the answer, the three harpooner boats
Were almost instantly manned and ready to be lowered.
But the Captain commanded, "Hold! Hold!"
And stood to his greatest height.
And called to another whaler
About what no one else had seen.
"Is that you, Tashtego. I see you have
Boats afloat." "I will standby, Captain."
Said Tashtego. The Harpooners of the other boats
Did not respond, They were too busy

14

Directing three boats toward the hugh gray-white
Flapping tail that fascinated these harpooners.
Suddenly there was chaos, and the great tail flapped
Down on one boat, and the boat was instantly empty,
And its occupants were no longer seen.
Then the recently excited Pequod crew suddenly
Gasped and froze. I expected that said, our ship's
Captain would continue the hunt,
But no, he and his ship slowly sailed away,
Leaving the empty harpoon boat adrift,
and its crew apparently dead.
Once again, I was impressed by
Captain Ahab's professionalism.
He waited silently for a long while, until,
One after another,
Four very yellow sailors popped to the surface.
The Pequod crew raised their arms and shouted,
"A miracle! A miracle!" and instantly lowered boats
To rescue the bobbing sailors. Our
Captain seemed pleased, as he calmly retired to his cabin.
I was puzzled, "Who are these men," I asked
Queequeg. "And why did their captain abandon them?"
Queequeg looked puzzled only briefly.
Then he answered, "They be probably stowaways,
Maybe Japanese, So their captain had to be
Loyalty to them, But Captain Ahab will always
Be loyal to the whaler's code. "Never abandon a sailor
At sea—"Never! Never!" Again, I was impressed by
Queequeg's knowledge, and how much his honor
Was like the Captain's. The naïve Manhattan
Sailor to be was slowly learning.

SCENE TWO: THE NARRATOR GAINS
FURTHER AWARENESS

I came to realize that this seemingly heartless whalers
Were in fact sadly sentimental when came to burying
A slaughtered whale. After they had pumped out the oil,
The corpse was tossed off ship to sink astern.
And although I heard no dirge being sung,
The solemn expressions on the hard faces
Of the sailors bespoke of profound grief.
Thus, while in life, the great whale's body
Might have been a terror to his foes,
In this world, his ghost became powerless our world.
But then I was reminded again that whalers are whalers.
"Sail ho!' came a triumphant voice from the main-mast.
Ahab suddenly erected himself, while thunder clouds
Were swept aside from his brow. That lively cry
From this deadly calm night might almost
Convert a better man. "Where away?"
"Three points to the starboard, sir,
And bringing down her breeze to us!"
"Better and better!" happily shouted Captain Ahab,
As he watched as, hand in hand, the ship and the breeze
Came on faster than the ship, and soon,
The Pequod began to rock. But Captain Ahab's
Eagerness to engage another whaler was dashed.
The other whaler soon disappeared beyond the horizon.
"Dash it! Dash it!" cursed the disappointed Ahab,
And he began morosely descending again
To his forlorn cabin. But then, Nimble as a cat,
Tashtego mounted aloft, And without altering
His erect posture, ran straight out upon the overhanging
Hoisting Tashtego, and he carried with him a light tackle,
Called a whip, when he continued on beyond
The end of sail-bar And off into the blue air
And down into ocean deep. "Man overboard!!"
Cried Daggo, who had quickly come

To his senses. "Tashtego is being dragged
Down o the ocean bottom!"
He yelled. Beginning to panic, Daggo yelled,
"Someone help! Someone help!" And Queequeg,
Heedless of his own safety, dived into the depths,
And clasping Tastego's seemingly lifeless hand,
Dragged him up to the surface. "Hooray! Hooray!"
Yelled all. And Queequeg, dragging the limp Tastego
To the deck, looked hardly brisk. And it seemed to me
That the as yet to be regular harpooner, Queequeg,
Had earned the respect of the crew, and maybe even
Ahab's. Then, for seeming months,
I felt it was smooth sailing For the Pequod,
Underneath the Cape of Good Hope,
With the Antarctic to the south, and the beginning
Off the great continent of Africa to the north.
And then such exotic places that I had longed to see:
Sumatra, Java, Bally, and Timor, and then on pass Sunda,
Malaca, and through the China Sea, and on pass to Australia
And onto the endless Pacific Ocean, where surely
There would an ocean full of oil rich-whales,
Even for revenge-hungry Captain Ahab,
And maybe even the *leg-crunching Moby Dick.*

And so, now Act One of Moby Dick has ended.
But don't let your imagination be suspended,
For what will happen in Act Two,
Will be even more splendid.

ACT II

SCENE I: THE NARRATOR SEES WHAT OTHERS SEE

Then, one day, all of us, but particularly
Captain Ahab seemed to see
A host of tantalizing vaporous spouts, urging us on.
And so, crowding all sails, Ahab pressed after them,
Urging the harpooners, handling their weapons
And loudly cheering from the heads of their suspended boats
That if the wind only held, little doubt had they
That they would capture a great number
Of these oil-rich treasures.
And Moby Dick might even be among
Them—or so Ahab hoped.

But alas, the great catch was not to be.
All of the whales out-sailed our slower Pequod,
Perhaps to be capture by some luckier whaler
And not the Pequod. "And I bet that Moby Dick was them,"
Mumbled Captain Ahab as he morosely
Began descending to his cabin.
But then he dashed back up. "Ship ahoy!
Hast how seen the white whale?" So cried Ahab,
Now hailing a ship showing English colors
Baring down under the stern. Trumpet to mouth,
The old man was standing in his hoisted quarter-boat,
His ivory leg plainly now revealed to the stranger captain
Who was carelessly reclining in his own boat's bow.
"Hast seen the white whale?" he asked.
"Seen you this?" and withdrawing it from the folds
That had hidden it, he held up a white arm
Of sperm whale bone, terminating
In a wooden head like a mallet.

"Man my boat!" cried Ahab, impetuously.
"Stand by to lower!" The English captain,

Hesitated only briefly. "I see! I see!"
Help the captain climb aboard, boys."
With his ivory arm thrust out in welcome,
The other captain advanced,
And Ahab, putting out his ivory leg, shouted,
"Let us shake bones together. And where
Did'st thou see The white whale, and how long ago?"
Pointing this ivory arm and sighting along it,
Toward the east, the other captain answered.
"And he took off that arm, did the hungry monster?"
Ahab asked. "Aye, he was the cause of it,
And your leg too, dare I remind you."
"Spin the yarn." Urged Ahab. How was it?"
"I was ignorant of the white whale at that time,
And here he comes bouncing from the bottom
O the sea with a milky white head and hump
And all crow's feet and wrinkled."
"It was he, it was he! cried Ahab, suddenly letting out his breath.
"And were there harpoons sticking near his
Starboard fin." Ahab asked.
"If they were, they were mine, they were mine!
But on, tell own." "Give me a chance then."
Said the Englishman, good neighborly.
Well, he was tangled in my line, and boiling in rage,
Spiriting away, dragging my ship with him."
So, I jumped into my first mate's boat
And, grabbing his harpoon,
I let the angry old man have!' since he saw
What I was going to do. But then, suddenly,
I was seeing nothing. I must have been slapped
With that wildly angry beast's pounding tail.
The next thing I knew, the whale-surgeon was
Telling me, "Tis a shocking bad wound, Captain,
And though I don't ordinarily advise it,
The ship's carpenter can carve you a new arm
Out of whale ivory." "And so it was done,"
Sighed the English Captain, speaking in
This characteristic English accent

"And what became of the whale?' demanded
Ahab impatiently. "Did'st thou cross his wake again?"
"Twice," declared the Captain.
"But could not fasten?" "Did not try.
No more white whales for me.
One lost limb is enough. But hark ye,
Don't you think he should be left alone?"
"Not by me!" Barked Captain
Ahab, as hurried to re-re-board his boat.
And then he shouted back at the polite
English Captain, "Which way was he headed again?"
The other captain pointed East.
And almost instantly, Ahab was standing erect in his boat,
Demanding of his harpoon from his harpooner,
Fedallah, "Then East it is!" Starbuck, the ever attentive
First mate realized That the oil cases
Were leaking in the ship's hole,
So, as was his wont, he went below to check.
Sure enough, there was considerable soaking the flowing.
So, he reported to the Captain's cabin to report this affair.
Hearing the footsteps on the stairs, the Captain shouted,
"Who's there, On deck, be gone!" "Captain Ahab,
It is I, Starbuck. The oil in the hole is leaking, sir,
And we must up Buttons, and break out ...."
"Up Buttons, and break out? Do we hold up and waste time
Tinkering with this Problem. "Either we do that, sir,
And waste in one day what we have come twenty
Thousand mile to gather. Isn't that worth saving, sir?
"So it is, so it is; if we first get it." "I'm speaking
Of the oil in the hole, Captain,' urged Starbuck.
"And I am not speaking of that at all. Begone!
Let it leak. I'm all a leak myself.
So, there are leaks in the oil casts.
There are always oil leaking casts in a whaler.
But there are far worse thing than leaky casts on the Pequod,
So we don't stop to stop any leaks." "But what about
The owners, sir?" "Let the owner stand on
Nantucket beach and yell typhoons. But look ye,

21

The real owner of a whaler is the captain.
And I'm the captain of this ship, and I say on deck!
On deck!" "Sir, stuttered the first mate, a lesser man than
I would back down ...." "Are you threaten to criticize
Your Captain! On deck! I say again."
"And I say, nay, not yet.
Should be not first try to understand one another?"
Ahab then seized a loaded musket from a rack and pointed it
Toward Starbuck, explaining, "There is one God that lords
Over the Earth, and one Captain that is lord over the
Pequod—And this captain says, On deck!"
From the fire in the eyes of the first mate, one might
Assume that he was ready face the blast
Of that canon-like weapon, but mastering his emotions,
He calmly started to quit the cabin, the pause, saying,
"Ahab, be aware of Ahab. Be aware of thy self, old man."
Ahab, watched him leave, and the said to himself,
"He waxes brave, but then obeys." Then, using the musket
As a cane, he passed back and fro, until he eventually
Replaced the weapon back on the shelf, and with an iron brow,
He rose to the deck, saying, "Thou art too good a fellow,
Starbuck." Then, raising his voice, he commanded,
"Furl the t'gallant-sail and close-reef the top-sail,
Fore and aft, and back the main-yard, and up Buttons,
And break out in the mail hole."
And so, all that the Captain said was done,
The leaky cases were to be sealed, as the
Captain almost secretly smiled.

When searching, they found that the casks in the hole
Were perfectly sound. So, the leak had to be deeper down.
It was dark and eerie down there, so this was a job
So someone indifferent to deep work and not inclined
To worry about unknown things. But even Queequeg
Would eventually succumb to illness from excessive effort.
And so began the noble and fearless descent into death.
To Ishmael, it seemed that his bosom friend had given up,
Was willing ready to float away into whatever elsewhere

22

His primitive religion called Heaven, or perhaps Hell.
Ishmael was heartbroken, this was his best friend,
The huge man who understood everything
And feared nothing.

But Queequeg just lay in his hammock,
Apparently waiting to die.
But, seemingly an afterthought, he ask the first-mate
To have the ship carpenter build him a coffin,
And it be made from the best available wood,
And of course large enough to contain his over sized body.
And even extra long harpoon. And so it was,
And since the whole crew so respected Queequeeg,
All demanded Queequeq's coffin would be almost royal,
Anyway, after all, he was a Prince.

But, when it seemed the end was near,
Queequeg brightened, and almost hopped
Out of his hammock. It was as though
The robust Queequeg had never been sick,
And he was ready and eager to crab up
His harpoon and stab a whale.
As an afterthought, Queequeg decided to use
His royal coffin and as his sea-chest.
So, it was a good thing it was long,
Queequeg's spear was to be stored in it.

And that great spear was soon to be used.
One morning, Captain came charging up from his cabin
Shouting "Oh, devilish tantalization of the gods!"

But Ahab's long awaited revenge was not for me.
We were sailing into the South Pacific where
Ahab was certain he would meet his nemesis, the
Hell fish, Moby Dick. But the South
Pacific was not Hell for me. It was Heaven.
It was where I, as I Manhattan youth, had expected

23

A pleasant cruise, but had experienced, instead,
Six months of spoiled rations, and endless boring sailing,
With a money hungry Merchant Captain,
Who was only forced by a near staring crew,
To land at the Bay of Nukualofa—my Paradise.
And it was a Paradise that was so alluring
That my shipmate Toby and decided to jump ship.
So, expecting to live off the land,
And so as to cause no suspicion,
We stuck few survival supplies in our pockets
And set off up jungle crevasse, heading toward the ledge
Overlooking Nukuheva Bay, expecting to be able to view
The money hungry xx merchant captain's vessel
When it set again out to sea. Yes, it did finally set out to sea,
Leaving two relieved and grateful merchant sailors
To send prayers to Davy Jones that we wouldn't have
to live with him if that old merchant
Ship had sunk into his realm.

But now, the true South Pacific isles were
Toby's and mine. The other side of the ledge
Was a tropical paradise, Yes, there were
Semi-naked young girls there to entice our fantasy,
Although not our reality, for their savage
Fathers would boil us up have us for dinner.
But the beauty of the landscape was
All we had ever hoped for
And it was still there—but it was not where
Ahab Hoped to meet his long awaited destiny,
So, I left my South Pacific fantasy and waited to serve
Ahab, a whale true sailor, a whaling ship
Sailor sailing with a whaler's mission:
Oil, and more oil, and more oil—
And the final revenge.

And Captain Ahab was *the* true whaler, who was again
Hoping for revenge "Stern all! Oh Moby Dick,
I clutch my heart at last!" Such were the sounds

24

That now came hurdling out of
The old man's tormented sleep.

The next morning the not-yet-subsided sea
Rolled in long slow billows of mighty bulk,
And striving in Pequod's gurgling track
Pushing her on like giant palms outspread.
And Ahab, apart from the others, and ever time
The ship pinched down her bowsprit,
He turned his eyes into the sun, and saw little,
And sought to challenge the sun to keep him from his quest.
But reigning in metaphoric thoughts,
He headed toward the helm.
Demanding how the ship was heading.
"East-sou-east, sir, said the frightened steersman.
"Thou liest!" smiting him with his clinched fist.
"Heading East at this hour of the morning,
And the sun astern?" Upon this, every soul
Was confounded, for the phenomena just
Observed by Ahab, Had unaccountably
Escaped everyone else, *The Pequod was heading
West, not East!* But then the old man laughed,
"I have it, It has happened before.
Last night, Mr. Starbuck, last night's thunder
Turned our compasses, that's all"
And then Captain Ahab strolled across the deck,
Looking smug, and his crew realized that
This was another Example of how this otherwise highly
Competent captain, Needed to be
recognized as a superior whaler.

But there was one way in which Captain Ahab's feelings
Were not self-serving, and the whole crew appreciated
What he did when little Pip, his much loved cabin boy,
Carelessly fell out of a ships-boat.
Laughing, he asked the crew, "Should we just
Let him float away and be eater by a shark,
Or maybe even by a whale we could spear and then be able

25

To pluck him out Of the hungry whale's belly?"
The crew laughed With him. "Well, I spect it
Would be easier if we just plucked
Him up now. And you know what?
I feel so sorry for little Pip,
That he will live in my cabin where he is less likely
To fall out of a boat and be eaten by a shark.
Anyway, he's so tiny, the shark probably wouldn't bother
To snack on him. So, haul him up, dry him up,
And set in a corner of the deck to finish drying."
And then the whole crew was pleasantly pleased
That their angry captain was occasionally happy after all.

Although Captain Ahab was unaccustomed
To using charts and instruments to determine the
Pequot's course, preferring to just his own innate skill,
This time he had checked those charts and was satisfied
His ship on the path toward the Equator.
The next day, a large ship, the Rachel, was decried,
Bearing directly down on the Pequot.
"She brings bad news, bad news," muttered one old sailor.
But Ahab's voice was heard over the muttering
"Have seen the White Whale?" "Aye, yesterday.
Have you seen a whale-boat adrift?"
Throbbing with joy, Ahab negatively answered,
And would have boarded the Rachel,
When he saw that its captain was already
Readying to board the Pequot. So, Ahab shouted,
"Where was he—Not killed!—Not killed!" he cried.
But this is the tale Rachel told. They had three whale-boats
In the water, when he saw the size of the white whale,
So, they lowed a forth boas, "In which was my son,
And another youngster of eleven years. . . ."
Then this forth boat, with strong rowing,
Came along the side of the tail that with of flip
Of that dreadful tail, the forth boat disappeared,
And as best the Rachel's captain could tell,
Was dashed to the bottom of the ocean,

And soon after the boat surfaced—without it occupants!
Then was desperation in the Captain's voice,
"My son, my son! For eight-and-forty hours,
Let me charter your boat. I will gladly pay whatever you ask."
But Ahab was looking away toward
Moby Dick must be waiting.
"Please, sir, answer me. My son, my son,
I must find him." But Ahab mere muttered to him,
"By this time, he's obviously dead."
"Follow him, my Pequod, he awaits my spear!"
Ahab shouted. "Away, we lose time."
And to the Rachel's desperate repeated plea of,
"Will you not help me!" Ahab merely replied,
"Nay, sir Captain, I have a White
Whale that awaits my angry spear."
And from that moment more, Ahab knew
Only his lust for revenge.
But, Flask, without his usually humor,
Was whispering to himself,
"It this were my dear son, I would allow
Moby Dick to devoir me,
If he would only give me back the son I have lost."

And then t there was another deadly encounter
With whale-dealt-death.
The whale ship Delight came along side Pequod.
"Have you seen the white whale!" bellowed Ahab.
"Seen, and now can show his work."
And then the Delight's captain
Quietly spoke, instructed his crew. "Are you ready, there?
Place the plank then one the rail and lift the body—
Oh God!" he cried, Advancing toward the
Hammock with uplift ed hands—
"May the resurrection and the life." He continued.
"Brace yourself. Up helm" cried Ahab,
Lightening up his men."
But the suddenly starting Pequod was not quick enough
To escape the sound of the splash that the corpse made

27

As it struck the sea; not so quick indeed, but that some of
The flying bubbles might have sprinkled the Pequot's hull
With ghostly baptism, as
Ahab hastily glided away from the
Delight In conspicuous relief.
"Ha! Look yonder! Look yonder!
Cried a foreboding voice in her wake,
"In vain, oh ye strangers,
Ye fly, ye fly away from our burial,
But as you leave us in you trail, see your own coffins".

The days were gray for a while, it was like sailing
On a slate sea, with nary a wave to ruffle the slickness,
And Starbuck saw the old man leaning over the rail,
And he seemed to hear his own heart slowly throbbing,
As did the captain's. But he was careful not to touch him,
Or be noticed by him, as he drew near.
Then Ahab turned anyway, "Starbuck!" "Sir." "Oh, Starbuck,
It is a mild, mild, wind, and mild looking sky.
On such a day, very much sweetness as this,
I struck my first whale, a boy harpooner of eighteen!
And now forty years, forty years of continued whaling
Forty years of privation and peril,
And I have not spent in those forty years, thee years at shore,
Oh what a fool old Ahab has been, oh God,.
Let me look not into the evil eyes of that awful whale,
Let me looking the eyes of my wife and my child,
And yes, Starbuck, I see my wife and my child in your eyes!"
"Oh my Captain, my captain! Noble soul! grand old heart,
Why should one give chase to that hated fish
In these deadly waters. I have wife and child too,
And mother and brothers, let us away this instant,
Let us alter the course. How cheerily, how hilariously,
Oh my Captain, how good to see old Nantucket.
But then the Captain had walk suddenly
Over to the other side of the deck as Parsee, the harpooner,
Was staring fixedly down into the slate gray sea,
What was there, what was there? I wondered.

What was that was washing away wife and child
From Ahab's now once again whale-tormented mind?

SCENE II: THE PLAY'S CLIMAX IN STAGES

Stage I days of calmness before the storm

All reminiscing aside, the chase was underway again.
The man of the Pequod mounted the mast
To look out for the white whale on the whales own ground
Where men would be swallowed mercilessly swallowed.
But we did not know this at that time.
Instead, the call when out, "There is Queegueg's coffin."
"A rather queer thing that," said Stuub.
"It was made a good enough one", said Flask.
This causal conversation went on for a while.
Then the Captain barked, "Enough of
This old women's chatter,
Bring up, nail down the lid, and cast it astern."

So, we sailed on, until the old man grew impatient,
Seemingly distrusting his crew's dedication to the kill.
"I will have first sight of the whale myself," he said.
But then he softened, "Take the ship, sir, I give it to you."
Then Captain ascended to top of the mast,
And seemed content for awhile just to stare at the sea.
"Then your hat, sir, your hat! Suddenly cried the
Sicilian seaman, who was posted at the
Mizzen-mask-head, behind Ahab,
For Ahab's hat had been blown away in the wind,
But it was dished out of the sea,
And that ended another day.

Stage II: the Chase Actually begins

"D'ye see him!" cried Ahab. "See nothing, sir"

"Turn up all hands and make sail! No more night resting."
"By salt ad hemp!" cried Stuub, but this swift motion
Of the deck creeps up one's legs and tingles at the heart.
This ship and I are two brave fellows.
We go with the gait and leave no dust behind!"
"Thar she blows!—she blows!—right ahead!"
Was now the mast-head cry. "Aye, aye!" cried Stubb,
I knew it—ye can't escape—blow on and split your spout,
Old whale! Ahab will dam off your blood!"
And Stubb was speaking for the rest of the crew as well.
The frenzy of the chase had by this time bubbling up.
Whatever pale fears and forebodings
Some of them might have felt before were now out of sight,
Because of their growing awe of Captain Ahab.
They had been separate sailors sailing alone at sea,
Now, because of their Captain, they were one, not thirty!
"Why sing ye not after him?" demanded Ahab,
But the sea had become calm again, as had all voices.
Nothing was near now but the forlorn songs of the seagulls.
But now sound blast forth again!

Stage III: Does a Real Chase now Begin?

"There she breaches! There she breaches!" was the cry
As in his immeasurable bravadoes, the White Whale
Tossed himself salmon-like to Heaven.
"Aye, breach your last to the sun, Moby Dick!' cried Ahab,
Thy hour and harpooning are at hand!"
Down, down, all of ye, but one man to the fore, The boats!—
Stand by!" Unmindful of the tedious
Rope-ladder of the shrouds,
The men, like shooting stars, slid to the deck,
While Ahab, less daringly, but still rapidly,
Was dropped from his personal perch.
"Lower away!" he cried as soon as he reached his boat.
"Mr. Starbuck, the ship is thine—keep it away
From the boats, but keep near them. Lower all!"
As if to strike terror into them, the whale,

Moby Dick had turned, and was now coming
At the three crews. Ahab's boat was central,
And cheering his men, he told them
He would take the whale head-on-head,
That is, pull straight up onto its forehead.
But the whale suddenly churned himself
Into a furious speed, almost at an instant,
Rushing among the boats with wide open jaws
And a thrashing tail, offering appalling battle
On every side, heedless of the irons darting at him
From every boat, seemingly only intent
On annihilating each separate plank of which
These boats were made. But skillfully maneuvering,
The boats for awhile eluded him,
While Ahab's unearthly slogan tore
Every other cry but his to shreds.
But now revenge-seeking Moby Dick
Seemed to cry his own slogan.
With a hellish cry that only a furious whale can make,
His massive, thrashing tail first shattered Daggo's
And then Flask's boat seemingly into sawdust.
Only Ahab's boat was still afloat, but the whale
Quickly took care of that. He angrily flipped
Ahab's boat over and over, until Ahab and his men
Found themselves underneath it, and struggling
To escape as if they were seals trying to escape
From turmoil battered sea-side cave.

As before. The attentive ship, having witnessed
The whole fight, again came bearing down
To pick up the floating marines and gear,
All to be deposited on the now trenched deck.
Now, as with Fedallah the day before, Ahab was
Fortunately, not so exhausted as the day before,
Was instead of standing by himself, although hung
Over Starbuck's shoulder, and the crew
Understood why, his ivory leg had been snapped off,
And all he had left was a sharp splinter.

"Aye, Starbuck, tis sweet to lean sometimes,
But I have now to lean more often now
Than any other learners in this perilous whaling trade."
"But no bones broken, I hope sir," Starbuck asked
With concern. "I tell you, yes, Starbuck. "I tell you yes,
And even what's left is shattered. Aloft there, which way"
"Dead to the leeward, sir." "Up helm, then pile on
All sails again. Boat-keeper! Down the rest of the boats
And rig them. Mr. Starbuck away toward the beast,
And now muster the rest of the boats crews.
Now give me anything to use as a cane. . . .
But I do not see Parsee, Oh pray God,
Don't let him be missing." Then all looked to the sea,
And Parsee was not seen, And as in a tragic play,
Ahab moaned, "What a man, the last I saw of him
He was piercing the beast with his harpoon.
Where is he, and where is the beast? Ahab shouted.
Then Starbuck grabbed the shaking Ahab,
"Great God! but for one single instance,
Show thy real self! Never, never will thy capture him.
In Jesus name, no more of this. We have failed
In all we've tried to do, still the unconquered beast
Laughs at us. Shall we keep chasing him
Until he swamps the last man? No more! Man,
No more! Moby Dick is forever, my gallant Captain."
But Ahab was not ready to end the fight.
"Gather round me, my heroic and fearless men,
And believe what I tell ye. Two days he has
Risen to the surface and floated, and tomorrow
Will be his third, and he will rise again,
But only to spout his last! Do ye feel brave, men?"
"As fearless fire!" cried Stubb. But Ahab
Had become practical again, "Starbuck,
Have the carpenter craft me another leg.
I will need it to mount the beast to pierce him
With his well earned death blow!"

ACT III

SCENE: THE FINAL BLOW

When dusk descended, the whale was still in sight
To the leeward, as was the broken keel
Of Ahab's wrecked boat, and since
Ahab's new ivory leg was fitted on him,
So was Ahab eager to go again.
So, as the new day was dawning, Ahab cried,
"Dye see him?" But the great whale was not in sight.
"So we follow! We follow!" Ahab encouraged his crew.
But the day ran on uneventfully, so Ahab demanded,
"Aloft there! What do you see?" "Nothing, sir."
"Nothing! and the noon at hand!"
"Oh my Lord, I've over chased him! I might have known,
With the harpoons he's towing. Toward him, toward him!"
"Against the wind, we now steers for that open jaw!"
Murmured Starbuck, but nevertheless, he followed the order.
"Stand by to sway me up!" shouted Ahab,
We should meet him soon." "Aye, aye, sir." Said Starbuck
And he straightway did Ahab's bidding,
And once more, the eager Ahab hung on high.
"Forward! Forward! I meet thee, this third time,
Moby Dick. But still the great whale came forward.
But suddenly Ahab became pensive, taking to Starbuck,
"I am old, Starbuck, hand me your hand
And shake hands with me, old friend, if it pleases you."
"It does, old Captain of mine," his hand tightening
The clasped hands as though with glue.
"My brave Captain, go not, go not!
But Ahab Ignored Starbuck again, and urged
His crew to assist him. Then another voice warned,"
The sharks, the sharks!, Come back, my Captain!"
But Ahab heard only his own voice
As he leaped into his boat. "Heart of wrought steel!"
Murmured the first-mate, Following with his eyes,

33

"Canst thou yet ring boldly to that sight.
Oh my God, what is this that shoots through me
And leaves me so deadly calm, yet expectant,
And my legs feel faint—Stir thy self, Starbuck.
Keep thy firmest eye on the boat!
And where's the old man now?
But Ahab was expecting what he next saw,
The whale had sounded, And Ahab,
Intending to be near him soon. But suddenly,
The water around him swelled in broad circles,
Then quickly up heaved, and preceded
By a raging sound, bedraggled by ropes and harpoons,
A vast form shot length wise into the air.
And then it hovered momentarily in the haze filled air,
Before slinking back into the deep. "Give way!
Shouted Ahab, as the whale's giant tail flapped about wildly,
Empting Ahab's boat, but leaving Ahab without a scar,
While on the ship, Daggo and Queequeg,
Who were stomping the blood stain planks,
Turned and saw that the whale
Had flipped over, and to crew's horror,
The half torn body of Parsee was seen,
With his sightless open eyes turned full on Ahab.
Then the harpoon dropped from Ahab's hand.
"Be fooled. Be fooled!" Then drawing a long lean breath,
He almost wept, "Parsee, I see thee again—
Aye, and thou goest before, but the beast
Will soon follow you!" Now, regaining his composure,
He shouted, "Who offers to jump into my boat with me?
Aye, I know you will, for you are not just men,
You are my arms and my leg one leg,
And I know you will obey me. But where is Moby Dick?
Has he gone down again?" "Oh, Ahab! cried Starbuck.
Not too late is it, even now, the third day, to desist!
See, Moby Dick seeks thee not. It is thou,
Thou, that madly seeks him!" But Ahab was ordering
Starbuck to follow the white whale's watery trail.
He also saw that his full crew was doing all that was needed

34

To have repaired boats ready to pursue the whale,
Tashtego, Queequeg, and Daggo all eager
To do their part to destroy Ahab's, and now their enemy.
Whether the agony of his being so viciously attacked,
Or whether he was just luring them on,
Moby Dick slowed, enabling his pursuers to near him.
"Sharks are coasting alongside us, sir." One man said.
Ahab noticed as well, "Tis not known whether
The wait to feast on us or the whale, can't be known.
I say, it is the whale, for I don't intend to be eaten."
Starbuck, following closely in the ship, believed
That he could see a smile on Captain Ahab's face.
Then Ahab asked his two oarsmen to assist him
To the helm of the boat, where he stood erect,
With his harpoon in his right fist, eagerly waiting.
Now the whale allowed the boat to come alongside.
Then he rolled over, and almost caused Ahab's boat
To roll as well, and Ahab was barely able
To avoid being spilled into the water,
Just as had happened to him the day before.
But it his oarsmen who were unprepared,
And who were flung out of the rocking boat.
But then, two of the oarsmen were able
To pull themselves into the boat again,
While the third, uninjured, was picked up
By the trailing ship. But the great whale suddenly
Suddenly turned on the small boat and attacked.
Ahab staggered, his hand slapping his forehead, cried out,
"I grow blind! Hands stretch out before me,
That I may know my way!. "The whale, the ship!'
Cried a cringing oarsman. But Ahab was too eager
To be concerned about the ship. "Dash on!, dash on!,
My men, I must go to the beast for this last time
To slide in my shaft and so bring an end
To my evil and noble enemy—or is he
My longtime friend?" But it was not just Ahab
Who was in this fight, on the ship,
Which had followed closely, Starbuck

35

Saw that the whale was now heading toward him.
"Oh ye sweet powers of air, hug me close.
Let me not abandon my duty.
Let me die trying to assist My Captain
In his great lifelong adventure
Of destroying his long lived archenemy!"
"The whale, the whale!" shouted Ahab.
"Stand not by me, stand under me!
Whoever you are who will help me.
And help Stub, or help him stay awake.
But I, atop my man, will toss my piercing spear,
Though it be my last, for my last is good enough!"
Then, look behind," he cried, "My ship! My Ship!"
For the whale had sunk beneath the Pequod
With all it non-boated crew, and Ahab's
Whaling memories. And then the ship,
Was sinking beneath the whale.
So, in horror and rage, Ahab sank his killing shaft
Into the near-dying Moby Dick,
So that soon dying whale would
Took all with him into the non-Christian death,
From which no one returns.
And thus, no *Amens* were needed.

RESCUE

But as the indifferent whale slowly sunk
And carried the Pequod and all of its crew
To the bottom of sea—Accept for one lonely orphan
of that whaling tragedy, And that was me, who,
Athough eventually rescued, would forever be haunted
By that whaling memory, and forever, in my dreams,
Be sailing the whaler Pequod on the churning sea.
And ironically, it was the whaler Rachel
Who Ahab had abandoned, who rescued me.

EPILOGUE

As spoken by the narrator

Captain Ahab, even though beyond death,
Continued to harpoon the thrashing whale.
But the indifferent whale merely sunk
And carried the Pequod and all of its crew
To the bottom of sea—Accept for one lonely orphan
of that whaling tragedy, and that was me, who,
although eventually rescued, would forever be haunted
By that whaling memory, and forever, in my dreams,
Be sailing the whaler Pequod on the churning sea.

Oh Poor Captain Ahab, he spent his too short life
Seeking revenge on an animal,
Although it was the great white whale,
And thereby inflicted upon his crew unending strife.
And thus I'm telling you this sad and oh so tragic whaling tale.
And so hear me now my rich and eager theater audience,
I hope you leave this theater
Believing that such vengeance makes no sense.

THE COUNT OF MONTE CRISTO

THE NARRATOR INTRODUCES THE PLAY

Young Dentes convinces the first mate
Of the Pharon to land on the Isle Elba,
So he can seek the help of Napoleon's
Doctor to treat his ship's beloved Captain.
Napoleon agrees to let his doctor
Treat Captain Leelere if Dentes
Will deliver a greeting letter to Napoleon's friend
When Dentes reaches Naples.
Dentes readily agrees, and then the novel
And Dentes' life takes its fateful course.

ACT I

SCENE I: DENTES VISITS HIS AILING FATHER

"Father, I had to report to my ship's owner
Monsieur Morrel, so now I was able to
Come to you. Father, you don't look well.
Have by eating? I've checked the icebox,
It's almost empty! Let me fix you something.
It's okay, son, I'm not hungry."
"Well, I'll fix something anyway, and I expect
It to be eaten when I come back later!
But now I've got to hurry, Mercedes
Will be dying to see me, and you know
How young women are. So, off I go Father."
The old man merely smiled weakly,
And waved his son along
But, as he did so, murmuring to himself,
"Farewell, loving son, I will see you again
Somewhere, somewhere, wherever that might be."

SCENE II: THE LOVERS EMBRACE!

Mercedes has been waiting breathlessly
For her childhood friend, now become her
Adult love. "Our love is too weak a word,"
She sighed. "He is my every breath,
My reason for living. Without him,
I would surely die!" "Oh, sister,"
Her brother protested. "You are not
A Character in some old spinster's novel.
You are a grown . . . well almost grown women.
Anyway, who is this poor, illiterate sailor?
He is not worthy of you. You need someone
Like my educated friend here, Fernand.

45

After Dentes sails off to sea again,
Coming back who knows when,
Fernand will be here doing what
A grown man should do,
Helping you to care for your many children,
And keeping you in a fine home,"
Saying this, the brother looked aside at Fernand,
Who seemed anything but the manly being
That the brother had been talking about.
He was more like a cringing child
Whose father had placed an undoable burden
On his whimpering son. "And yet,"
The brother thought, "there was something stronger
Hidden in that weakling." When Fernand risked a look
At Mercedes, lust peeked through,
Lust and the willingness to do anything
To capture the love of this lovely maiden.
The brother, looked away, somewhat confused.
"Or perhaps an even more suitable husband—
Look here at the first mate of the Pharon.
Look at this more mature man, Captain Danglars.
Wouldn't he make a wonderful father
Of all my many nephews?"
But then Dentes burst into the room.
"Oh Mercedes, will you forgive me?
I was detained by my ship's owner,
Monsieur Murrel, and would you believe this?
He is making me the new Captain
Of his good ship, Pharaoh!" Fernand
Was too lost in his fearful fantasies to notice,
But the brother was aghast, and Danglers
Looked furious, and in an aside to the theater
Audience, Danglers voiced that anger.
"Never! That foolish young boy
Will die by my knife before that happens!

46

SCENE III: THE PLOT

Danglar's eyes followed the enraptured couple
As they disappeared around the corner
And on into another more secluded part of the house.
Then he noticed that Fernand had slipped
Back into his chair, pail and trembling.
He also noticed that Caderousse, his too often tipsy friend,
Had come into the room, singing
One of their old drinking songs, but Caderousse
Then became sad. "So, my good sirs, I see not
Everyone is happy." "I am in despair," said Fernand,
Head still bowed. "Well, I'll say that I am annoyed
That the lucky new and very young ship Captain Dentes
Will no doubt more money now
To pay the debt on his father's old house,
And I can't foreclose on the mortgage."
But Danglars turned his sharp gaze
Onto Fernand, "And what are you going
To do about your despair, sit there
And tear out your hair? Is that how a future Count
Is suppose to behave?" "But what else can I do?"
Fernand complained. "You can stop complaining!"
Shouted Danglars "As the saying goes,
Seek and ye shall find." And I have sought,
And I have found, I have found
That I want to sink my knife into that new Captain
Until he sinks to the bottom of the sea!"
The brother, startled at this outrage, cautioned
"I understand your fury, but you must remember
The enchanting Mademoiselle Mersedes says
That if Dentes is harmed, she will kill herself.
"Yes, yes, and I do despair for her, but I do swear
By all the gods at sea, that Dentes has to die?
But then Danglars became thoughtful, and again,
And he muttered softly to himself,
"But what if Dentes does not die?

47

Then he lifted Fernand's head and whispered
In his ear, "Good friend of mine, I believe
There a way for the so called Captain Dentes
To merely go away without dying.
Wouldn't that get you what you want,
Mercedes love, you, or at least her hand in marriage?"
"But how, but how can I do that, I beg of you?"
"Don't beg, my friend, just listen to what your
Clever friend has to say." Fernand became
More alert then, and whispered back at Danglars,
"I know that you have some personal anger
Against Dentes, so tell me how
We can both gain from not killing Dentes."
"No, not tell you, show you how clever we can be.
"In that drawer over there," he directed Caderousse,
Who had almost passed out, "See that drawer over
There. I'm sure there is Pencil and paper.
Yes, that's it. Now Caderousse, in your not so clear
Left-handed script, write what I tell you.
"It has come to my attention that the new first mate
Of the Pharon, Before coming home to Marseille,
First landed On the Isle of Elba, where he met, in secret,
With the evil Emperor, Napoleon,
Who gave him a message to deliver
To an unknown man in Marseille.
I Bring this your attention in all confidence,
For Dentes is my friend, and I wish him no harm.
Now, Caderousse, also in confidence,
Get this document to the Crown Prosecutor,
And we will let your and friend Denten's fate take its course."
And with this, Danglars couldn't hold back his anger.
He no longer whispered, he shouted!
"Not my ship! Not my my ship!"

SCENE IV: THE BETROTHAL, GONE BAD

The next day, the weather was fine.
The sun rose, brilliant and clear,
And its purple rays glistened like
Rubies on the foamy crest of the waves.
At least that was the way the happy sailor,
Dentes, experienced his life as he
Waited impatiently for the betrothal meal
To be served in this elegant French restaurant.
The meal was due to begin only at noon,
But the room was partially filled
By a few of Dentes fellow sailors
From his ship Pharon, all in their very best
Dress uniforms in honor of the engaged couple.
Would be joining the celebrating couple.
And that is just what happened,
And seeing the owner, Monsieur Murrel
Entering, the crew shouted "Hurrah!"
Next to enter the restaurant were
Mercedes and four of her friends,
Where upon, Dentes took her arm
And led her into the dinning hall.
Finally, there came Dentes' old father,
Followed by Fernand, with his sour smile
That neither Mercedes nor Dentes could see.
The ecstatic couple could see nothing
But one another. Danglars and Caderousse,
Having discharged their clandestine mission,
Danglers exchanged warm and energetic handshakes
With Dentes, who thanked his first former first mate
For attending the happy ceremony.
Danglars had to force a smile at Dentes'
Use of the term, first mate.
"That won't be happening ever again,
My young ship Captain," he muttered, but he,
Nevertheless, managed to maintain his smile.

Then Mercedes motioned to Fernand, and stated,
"You have been like a brother to me,
So sit by my left side, as Dentes, my love
Will sit on my right side."
She spoke with such softness that it
Struck Fernand like a blow from a dagger
To the depths of his soul. Danglars noticed
Fernand's private agony, and he smiled
Another of his conspiratorial smiles,
While muttering aside, "Just you wait, you'll
Get your revenge, friend Fernand." But again,
Dentes was too involved in his own
Pre-marriage nervousness, declared to Mercedes
"How could I possibly be the husband of
This perfect maiden?" At which, Mercedes blushed.
But then Caderousse took up the task of
Secretly laughing at the bride groom,"
"Well now, husband, or not yet husband,
And now Captain Dentes," Caderousse laughed.
"Try behaving like a husband now,
And see how she treats you!" Mercedes
Blushed again. Dentes then looked at his watch,
"But in an hour, she will be, and I will be
The proudest husband in all of France!"
Danglars smiled his conspiratorial smile again,
Muttering to himself, "There will be
Little to be proud about where you will soon
Be going." But then a dull sound echoed
From the outside hallway, and the sound
Of heavy footsteps broke into the previously gay
Dining hall, gaining everyone's attention,
And bringing deadly silence to the room.
A commanding voice barked, "This is the law!
Is there a sailor named Dentes in this room?"
Dentes struggle to his feet, as Mercedes
Tried to hold him back. "Yes," Dentes
Spoke softly, and then gathered his dignity,
"Yes, I am Captain Edmond Dentes, what do want

With me." The law officer almost shouted,
"I arrest you in the name of the law!
Step forward that I might cuff you!'
"What, what?" demanded Mr. Murrel,
"There must be some mistake. This is
My ship's Captain, you can't do this!"
The law officer then realized that
Mr. Morel was someone important,
And he modified his tone. "I appreciate
Your concern, sir, but I have my duty,
Please take up your concern with my commander,
The Deputy Crown Prosecutor But now,
I must do my duty. Once again, Captain Dentes,
Step forward, so I might cuff you!"
Dentes, who had now regained his dignity,
Did as asked, was cuffed and led down
The stairway and into an iron-bared wagon.
And there was a resounded clang
As the door banged shut behind him.
And was suddenly dark all around Dentes,
Blotting out, seeming forever,
The formerly gay dinning hall.
Dentes could not hear her, but he knew
That his beloved wife-to-be must be sobbing,
And her brother and Fernand were there
To dry her tears. But he didn't see the
Triumphant grins in Caderousse's and Dangler's faces.

SCENE V: THE DEPUTY CROWN PROSECUTOR.

Gerard de Villefort was at this moment
The happiest as it is possible for a man to be
At the age of twenty-six, wealthy in his own right,
Married to a wealthy and beautiful women,
And now a Deputy Crown Prosecutor
Of France. But so much for this unseemly pride,

51

"I must to my duty. The Police Commissioner
Was waiting to be addressed, and now he did so.
"I am here, Mr. Prosecutor.
And I have read the letter slipped to you
From some secret source. "You did well
To arrest this man, said the Prosecutor. Now tell me
Everything you know of him and the conspiracy."
"About the conspiracy," "I know nothing, but all the papers
That were concealed on him are on your desk,
Unopened." Then the Prosecutor asked further,
"This Dentes, did he serve in the Navy Before joining
The Merchant Marines?" "No, my Lord, he is quite young,
About nineteen." It was at this moment that Dentes
Was shoved into the room. flustered, but trying
To remain calm, He spoke courteously, "Sir, I have
Come here . . ." "Brought here!" interrupted
The Police Commissioner. "Yes, brought here, **Sir,**
And I don't know why." The Prosecutor said calmly
"Then tell me who you are, and when I fully understand
The situation, I will tell you why." "Yes sir,"
Dantes snapped to attention "I am Edmond Dentes,
Sir, the Captain of Monsieur Morel's ship, Pharon."
"And how old are you?" "Nineteen, sir,"
Dantes answered in a now firmer voice.
The Prosecutor's voice was now softener,
"Tell me all I need to know to best
Understand your situation. But I must warn you,
I know very little about why you are here.
But I do wonder about this. Did you serve
Under the Usurper" "I was about to
Enroll in the Navy, when he fell."
"And your opinion about the legitimacy
Of Napoleon's leadership?" "I must confess,
Sir, I am not sophisticated about political matters.
All I know for certain is that I love my father,
I respect Mr. Morel, and I adore my fiancé,
Mercedes, and I can't wait to marry her!"
The Prosecutor couldn't help feeling

A little warm on hearing this young man's
Enthusiastic response. "And I commend your
Commitment. But I must continue my inquiry.
Do you know of any enemies you might have?'
"Enemies? I am of too little importance
To have any enemies, although my
First mate on the Pharon, Danglars,
Often fussed at me for being too playful
With the crew members who served under me"
On hearing this, the Prosecutors became
Even more relaxed. "That hardly seems a crime,
Young Dentes. So, let's get to the unpleasant
Reason why you are here. He took out
A letter and put it on his desk.
This is what brought you here. Do you recognize it?"
"No Sir, but it seems intelligent, but I know
Nothing about what it might say,
Since I cannot read. But I am please
That whoever wrote this must be
Very smart, and such a smart person
Thinks me important enough to be
His enemy." Dentes was smiling now,
And the Prosecutors was smiling as well.
"And now there is this question.
Before arriving at Marseille, did you not
Briefly land on Elba, and why was that?
And did you not meet Napoleon
And why was that, and what took place
At that meeting?" "I needed Neapolitan's
Approval to use his doctor to treat
My ailing Captain." "And did he give that
Permission?" "He did, but it was too late.
My Captain died soon after" "Sorry, young sailor,
And what else took place at that meeting?"
"Napoleon and I had made a bargain. I would give
His permission to use his doctor,
But I must agree to carry a greeting
To his friend at Marseille" "And what

Did this message say?" "I do not know, Sir
Dentes took and envelope out of his vest,
And placed in on the desk, "You can see
That it is sealed, and anyway, you remember,
I can't read." The Prosecutors examined
The letter, and seemed satisfied.
"Well, that about sums it up, I will
Destroy this letter." And he prepared
To toss it into the fireplace.
Dentes sighed, "Then I can leave?
I have to get back to my betrothal party."
"Yes, by all means, go, and enjoy your party."
But Dentes was barely out of the room,
When the Commissioner collapsed his head
In his hands on his desk. Then, rising his head again,
He shouted, "That's it! That's it!, this letter,
Thank God I didn't toss it into the fireplace.
This letter will make my fortune!"
Then he quickly called the Police Commissioner
Into the room, and instructed what to do
About their prisoner. Dentes understood nothing
But he dutifully allowed the Police Commissioner
To shove him from the room, After his office door closed,
He gleefully began planning his next move.

At the bottom of the stairs outside the Commissioner's
Office, the Police Commissioner gestured to two gendarmes,
Who took up their positions on either side of Dentes
And shoved him into an iron caged wagon,
Then he was taken from that cage, and put
Into another cage, which since it rocked,
It must be on a small boat. For a while, he knew
Nothing, but from the noise and rocking of the boat,
He must be in Marseille harbor,
And he was instantly happy. This was where his
Own ship's boat had deposited him
When he was on his way to meet beloved Mercedes.
But the boat continued on passed the Battery,

And this direction Dentes could not understand.
"But where are you taking me?" he asked.
"We are not allowed to tell you,. But you
Will know soon enough." Still, he was not
Too worried. He saw nothing but open sea ahead,
So maybe they were going to deposit him
On the beach, and he could be on his way to Mercedes.
But no, they were continuing on out to the open sea.
Now Dentes was becoming desperate,
"As fellow French soldiers, please show me
The respect that we always show our fellow soldiers,
Where are you taking me?" One of the gendarmes
Looked at the other Gendarme and shaking his head,
He quietly whispered. "See you not that black rock?
That, my poor friend, is Chateau d'IF."
Dentes shuttered, "You can't be taking me there.
This is a prison for only major political prisoners,
And I have committed no such crimes!"
The gendarme was sympathetic, but he
Clutched Dentes tightly when his prisoner
Tried to jump out of the boat. Then a voice called out
From above, "Where is the prisoner?" "Here,"
One of the Gendarmes replied. "Good, then release him
To follow me." Dentes, was now resigned
To his undeserved but terrible fate.
Then they took him to a small room.
"This is your room for the night,"
He was informed. "The Prison Governor
Has gone to bed, so he will reassign you
To your permanent room in the morning.
Meanwhile, here is bread and water.
This is all you can expect while you are here."
Dentes believed his could hear a smile
On that darkened face, murmuring,
"As long as you are here,"
Then Dentes shuttered and slumped to the damp floor
And whispered to himself that he was being

Forever condemned to a metaphorical Hell.
But he was soon to realize that this
Was to be his condemnation to what was to be
An endless non-metaphorical Hell.

ACT II

SCENE I: THE LAST EVENING OF THE BETROTHAL

The aristocracy had gathered in one of the best
Homes in Marseille. Villefort rushed in hurriedly
But obviously pleased. "Sorry to have missed
The party, but I had serious business,
Which is now successfully completed,
But now I have even more urgent business
In Paris, with the King, or at least with his agents.
So, away I go, and my apologies again.
And he hurried out again, pleased to there
the gasps of the party guests. "Well you might be
Surprised," he whispered, smiling.
At the front gate, he saw a pale ghost-like
Figure, upright and motionless in the shadows.
It was the lovely young Mercedes who was
Desperate to know why her fiance had been arrested.
"The man of whom you speak," he answered
Briskly, "is a major criminal, and I can do nothing
For him, Mademoiselle." Mercedes could not
Suppress a sob, but she tried to stop him.
"At least tell me where he is, so I can
Seek to know if h is alive or dead."
"I don't know, Mademoiselle. He is no longer
My responsibility," and he hurried past
Mercedes, leaving her in despair.
Seeing Mercedes that way reached into
Some part of Villefort that could still feel
Regret or even some shame at what
He had done to the totally innocent Dentes.
But he shoved those feeling aside.
Muttering, he explained to himself,
"I have a right to reward myself,
As I also serve France." But in some part of his body,
He saw the unfortunate Dentes

Awaiting further descent in to Hell—
The deepest Dungeon of the Chateu d'IF

SCENE II MERCEDES ASSUMES AT LEAST A LITTLE CONTROL

For Mercedes, this was the end of her life.
Her precious Dentes was imprisoned for life
So all she could do was return to the room
That Dentes's father had provided for her
And wait to die alone. But it a came to her
That she was not alone. She felt her mainly swollen belly
There was a part her that would soon also be Dentes.
Then there was knock on her door, and Fernand
Looking, as always, when he approached her
Eager but hopeless, but what happened next
Totally surprised him. Beautiful, desirable
And unobtainable, jump from her bed
And through herself into his arms.
"Oh my always faithful friend, Fernand,
That you for coming to my aid.
After I have had time to pull myself together,
I want to spend more time with you.
Would that be okay with you?"
"Okay!", Fernand gasped. "I am yours forever.
Today, tomorrow, and right now
If you will have me!" "Thank you, my precious friend,
But now I have to gain control of my feelings.
Perhaps next week will be time enough."
From the look on Fernand's, Mercedes knew
That she had accomplished what she needed to do.
Now she would just have to shove down her guilt
At having deceived Fernand. At least he would be
Happy, and she would have to, somehow,
Suppress her eternal grief. There could never
True happiness without Dentes, but partial

Happiness with what she would have of him
Would have to do.

SCENE III: THE CHATEU D'IF—REAL HELL

Dentes realized the cell down below
Was the dungeon. As the iron bars clanged
Behind him, and the gray darkness closed in on him,
He finally accepted his fate, the Hell
That the seemingly kind Inspector had condemned him.
Not only was he caged in, he still had chains
On his ankles. His fine party clothes
Would not be cover enough to protect him
From the damp air that surrounded him.
He shuttered, but the small energy that required,
Didn't warm him at and, shuddering again,
He flopped down on the wet floor
And curled up into a fetal position,
And began to weep. After a short time thought,
A modicum of self-respect took hold of him.
"You are not a child, Dentes. No you are not
Going to be the proud Captain of the Pharon,
But you are still Dentes, the successful
Merchant sailor who fellow sailor liked
And respected him so, Dentes, you can
Make the best of this. Having reassured himself,
He struggled to come to his feet.
Looking up, far up there was a hint of light.
True, it was a gray light, but was probably
Because it was a cloudy day. But that self-deception
Did little to lighten him mood.
It had been a sunny day when he was brought her,
And it was going to be one long, cold, damp
Gray day until, in who knows how many years,
Before he again saw sunlight.
So, he crashed again to the floor

And assumed his fetal position. It would take
A miracle to make him a man again.

And what he experienced the next day,
Only reinforced that feeling.
"Ah, what do I call you, not Captain,
Not even sailor. No, you are prisoner number ..."
He turned to one of the guards, "What is his number?
I forget." The guard shook his head.
"But commissioner, we have so few prisoners,
Let's just name him Prisoner X." "Good"
Said the Commissioner, "Well my special
Prisoner X, let me introduce you too
A special ritual you will experience
On the anniversary of your entrance
Into our special facility." His voice remained
Mock polite, but nevertheless commanding.
"Strip off that fine, though damp blouse,
Guard, his chains should be loose enough
So he can lean against the wall.
Sorry it's so damp and slippery.
But careful not to fall down."
Dentes heard a sound he hadn't heard before.
But he knew that it leather whip
Being withdrawn from the Commissioner's belt.
And even before he heard it, he knew
It was the sound of flesh being ripped from his back . . .
Or was it sound of his almost infantile voice
Crying out, "No, please no!" but that only
Increased the intensity of the lashes,
Until he slumped into blackness.
But it was not a peaceful unconsciousness,
It was the sleep that would hold nightmares
Of daily desperation, waiting for his next
Anniversary with the commissioner.
And the unconscious Dentes knew
That, in between times, who knows what even
Greater horrors awaited him?

SCENE IV: SAME CAN BE EVEN WORSE THAN PAIN

The pain of the sameness was not just
In the cold and discomfort, but also
In the waiting, fearfully for what was going
To happen next, so he was surprised that
What happened next was not painful.
One of his gendarme came into his cell
And tossed clean prison clothes in his face.
"Here, ware these and come with me,"
He ordered. No, fool, let me first undo your chains."
The gendarme then marched Dentes up stares
Into a room that was so bright that,
At first, Dentes couldn't see. "Sit here,"
He was commanded. Then the gendarme left the room.
Next, Dentes heard hushed voices
Behind the far wall. He rushed to lean
His ear against the wall so he could hear better.
The voices became clearer. "Prisoner, I am the new
Governor General of this prison,
And I want to know who are my prisoners are,
So, who are you?" The voice that replied
Was not disrespectful, but neither was it respectful.
Dentes had heard that accent before,
And it sounded Italian. "As you know doubt know,
I am Father Abbe Faria. And prior to my conversion
To the cloth, was a warrior, and a damn good one,
But pardon my language." Dentes thought aloud
"Is that a smile I hear in the Father Abbe's voice."
"And was it your warrioring that got you into this prison?"
"No, it was my failure to fight for King Louise.
But by then, I was through with fighting.,
So I guess that made me a traitor."
This time, the voiced sounded annoyed.
"Or perhaps it was your disrespect
For a French officer of high rank."
The Governor General was obviously annoyed,

"Send him back to his cell," he barked, "And send in
The next prisoner." His voice was now indifferent.
There was the shuffling of feet,
And Dentes hurried back to his seat across the room
After that, Dentes' questioning
Was what he expected. So he said what
He had said before, insisting that he was innocent,
And of course, the new Governor General
Indifferently ignored him, and he was sent
Back his dungeon. But, to his surprise,
He was left in his dark, damp jail cell,
With clean clothes, and no longer chained.
"Maybe there was a God in this Hell after all."

But when, soon after, it was time
For his annual visit from the prison's Governor,
Hell, God wasn't in this Hell, he knew now.
The swishing whip whispered its painful message,
And Dentes begged forgiveness of his sin
Of assuming innocents, and even of being human.
Unconsciousness was to be his eventual forgiveness.
He assumed his ritual fetal position,
And when he eventually awakened,
He put back on his new, clean prison shirt.
Then, when his mind cleared a bit,
He wondered why he hadn't been cold without his shirt.
Could it have been because his prison meals
Provided him with energy to keep him warm?
Maybe, but he reminded himself that,
Since the prison food was delivered once a month,
And only in the first of the month, did he get
Larger portions, before the food spoiled.
At the end of each month, he was forced
To eat the spoiled food, which he did.
So maybe that explained his warmth.

Fortunately, his food explaining didn't
Explain away the pain of the annual whipping.

But another thought did help a bit.
He was becoming so angry at the Prison Governor's
Smirking before he applied the lashes,
That maybe the heat and his anger gave him some warmth.
So, he held on to a dream he was developing,
That someday, he would have his revenge.

It was several years later that his day-dreaming of revenge
Was interrupted by what he thought was scratching sound.
It seemed to be coming from the wall upon which
His head was leaning. It was probably one of those
Giant rats he had heard scamper in the corridor outside his cell.
Boy, they were big, and although the thought disgusted him,
If he was hungry enough, he would eat one—
Lots of protein, he thought. But when the scratching
Started again, he leaned closer to better listen.
But then the sound ceased. But the next morning, it began again.
So, he scratched back and, low and behold,
The scratching became louder, and more rapid.
So, Dentes scratched even harder.
And this went on all afternoon, and into the evening,
When the gendarme slide his pot of food underneath
The cell door. And Dentes started to eat, the scratching stoped.
Perhaps the scratcher had also stopped to eat.
But, to Distain's disappointment, it didn't start again.
Well, perhaps the scratcher was older,
And more easily tired. Then Dentes remembered
The Father Abbe he had heard being interviewed
Several years ago. No doubt that man was considerably
Older than Dentes, Dentes realized.
So, he would be patient. And that patience
Paid off. The next day, a scratching recommenced.
And for the first time in Destin's long imprisonment,
The possibility of hope in this Hell blossomed.

The next morning, after the guard had slipped
His tray of food through the flapping lid
Beneath the door, the scraping recommenced

In earnest, but Dentes then realized
That the scratching had been just a signal. Now an even louder
Banging began beneath one slab of stone on the floor.
The banging went on until late evening,
When the guard took away Dentine's feces bucket.
After that, too little light filtered in from beneath
The cell door for the work to continue.
At least, that's what Dentes assumed,
Since he had not heard speech from the banger.
What happened at about ten o'clock next morning,
Turned Dentes's expectation into joy.
A large stone slab in the middle of the cell popped up
And fell over, and slowly there emerged from the opening
A gray head of hair, and then two eyes,
Followed by a smiling face. "May I come in, young man?"
Asked a gentle Italian accented voice.
Dentes gasped, "Yes, yes, Abbe . . . Fa ...
By all means." The short man, who was also shrunken,
Dragged himself from the hole. Dentes hesitated
But a moment, and then rushed forward and hugged the man.
"Yes, yes, I needed that too," the Father said,
But let me look at you. Skinny, I see, but one who must have
Once been, lean and strong. Much taller than me,
But nevertheless, one who will be capable
Of digging along with me, and this time in the right direction.
I have now spent maybe nine years tunneling
In the wrong direction, thinking I was going
To reach the wall overlooking the sea.
So you and I will now begin tunneling
In the opposite direction . . . to freedom!"
"To freedom!" parroted Dentes.
But I will need an iron bar like yours.
There nothing but stone wall in my cell."
"I found this in an even deeper cell that must have been dug
When the prison was being built. Construction
Material was left there, and now these bars
Will be our digging tools." The Abbe looked at Dentes,
And smiled, "And maybe something else."

Then Dentes followed Abbe down the hole,
And to Dentes surprise, Abbe was holding
Ahead of him, a small torch with which
He guided the way. Eventually they came
To a room that was much larger than Dentes's.
"Wow!" Dentes shouted, though quietly,
You are obviously are more important than I am."
"And richer," Abbe gave one of his enigmatic smiles.
"Or so they hoped, but make yourself comfortable"
The first thing that Dentes did was sit softly
On a straight backed chair, then all he could do was sigh.
After a moment though, he studied the room.
There was a simple bed, a side table with a stand
For a torch, a desk, and stacks upon stacks of books.
Since Dentes couldn't read, he assumed
Many of these large books must be about religious subjects,
But he could only guess what else.
"Would you like to read one?" he asked
Offering a book. Dentes could only be embarrassed.
"I can't read," he whispered, and the Abbe
Seemed to suppress a look of surprise,
But then the smile and said gently, "Well,
We'll have to do something about, won't we?
"Yes, please," was all that Dentes could say.
"But more tunneling first," the Abbe became
Stern. "You will have to earn your schooling!"

And so the learning began. At first,
Most of the learning was about how Abbe
Tunneled most effectively while lying on his stomach
And crawling forward, while somehow keeping
His small torch lit. After a time, Dentes
Took the lead, and since he was stronger,
They made faster progress. This pleased Abbe,
So he gave more time to Dentes's book learning.
He introduce Dentes to subjects Dentes
Didn't even know existed, and certainly didn't know
What they meant. "What weird words you're saying,

I've never heard words like, Economics, or Mechanics,
Or Astronomy." "Well soon enough," Father Abbe said,
And you will not only know the meaning of the subjects
I'm talking about, you will be reading books about
These strange subjects." Dentes could only shake his head
Doubtfully, but his respect for Abbe was growing so rapidly,
He found himself believing what he was being told.
And when they soon launched into his military training,
Dentes was often banged about by Abbe's
Swift and accurate sword play—
No swords, of course, but slabs of hard wood
From the bottom of Father Abbe's bed.
"You've got to swing quickly to block my blows
And a lot more quickly if you ever expect
To punish me like I'm punishing you."
"But I don't want to punish you, Abbe,
You're a priest . . . and my friend."
"Well this friend is going to bloody your bottom,
If you don't treat me like your enemy.
What say to this? Think of me as you friend,
The Prison General, and see if you can
Swing faster, and maybe even harder."
To Dentes amazement, he slammed
The mock sword against Abbe's shoulder.
Then Abbe backed away quickly,
And merely smiled. But then he slammed back
Even harder, and Dentes didn't smile, at first,
But then he swung even harder,
But again made no contact, he smiled—
Hee was learning! Thank Whatever Above, he was learning!

Now, Dentes began to pride himself
As he became better avoiding,
And sometimes even delivering blows . . .
Until it occurred to him that his swordplay improvement
Was less his doing than it was because of
Abbe's growing weakness. And this was
Even more noticeable in their laborious

Crawling through their lengthening tunnel,
Abbe stopped and groaned. "Sir, what's happening?"
Dentes asked. Let me take the lead." After a moment,
The priest took a sharp breath, and moved on.
Now, this stopping became the habit,
Until, without asking, Dentes took the lead.
But soon, this didn't help, Abbe lagged behind,
And they had to discontinue tunneling.
Finally, the priest had to admit
He was no longer able to continue.
"In fact, my son, we have to accept,
That even if I had more time,
We cannot reach to seaside wall.
It is time for me to reveal how I now feel.
Frankly, I am glad to accept my end."
"Accept your end! No, Father, no!
We, together, will reach freedom,
And then we will seek the great treasure
You've told me about . . ." "Ah yes, the treasure,"
Now Dentes was certain that
He could see a smile on the priest's face.
"Yes you indeed will seek and find the treasure,
But I will be wherever the cruel prison governor
Dumps me." "Dumps you?" Dentes was horrified,
He couldn't accept that even the disrespectful
Governor would treat this saintly priest in such a way.
"Besides, Father Abbe you are not going to die,
No, no, no, you are not going to die!." And Dentes buried his face
In his father's chest. Abbe patted him companionly,
"It's okay, son, let me rest now. We will
Talk about this tomorrow." Dentes reluctantly agreed.
"Yes, tomorrow sir." and he lay down on the hard stone
Next to the priest's bed. It was a fitful night for Dentes.
He kept waking up, and listened the priest's
Shallow breathing . . . until it stopped all together!
Dentes spring up and arched over the priest.
Laying his ear to Father Abbe's chest.
But try as he might, he could hear no heart beat.

He pulled back and started to wail . . .
But then he caught himself. "No, this is not the way
My respected Father would expect me to behave.
His mind shifted into practicality. "No, my father
Would expect me to plan how to escape this
Inhuman prison, so I could fulfill our dream.,
"Yes, you won't be with me, Father,
But I will use the half of the cloth bag you gave me,
And from my mind, add the other half,
And I will find our treasure. And I will use it,
To honor what you have done for me . . .
And somehow get my revenge!"

And so, rather quickly, to his surprise,
He came up with a plan. He left the priest's body
In disarray, although he would have liked
To have arranged his body as though
It was in a holy coffin. Then he returned
To his own cell, and waited for the guard
To find Abbe's body. Through the wall,
He heard what he knew was two gendarme's
Returning with the Prison Governor.
"Look again!" the governor demanded!"
That map has to me here somewhere."
But they were unsuccessful, and Dentes knew why.
He had one half of the map stuffed in his pocket,
And the other half hidden in his mind.
And they had no idea that Dentes and the priest
Even knew each other. "Ah, ha, the plan progresses."
He then heard the priest's body being folded
Into a canvases shroud, and tied in, to be carried away.
Dentes quickly crawled through the tunnel,
And it was easy to stay back far enough
To avoid being seen. Then he heard
The Prison Governor and the two gendarmes walk away.
He didn't know why, perhaps they needed other burial goods,
But he took advantage of his luck. He dashed ahead,
Unfastened the shroud, dragged the priest

Back down the corridor, and tied himself into the shroud,
Held his breath, and waited impatiently.
He held his breath even tighter, when the gendarmes
Picked him up to carry him to the cliff overlooking the ocean.
"Hey," one of the guards complained,
How could this frail old man weigh so much?"
"Stop complaining. The Prison Governor barked.
He probably swallowed all that gold,"
The Governor quipped bitterly.
Then Dentes could feel the two guards
Swinging him back and forth,
As the gendarmes prepared to toss him into the ocean.
Without thinking, Dentes couldn't resist.
He loosened the ties On his shroud and peered out.
What he saw almost cause him to shout with joy.
No, it wasn't the sky, which he hadn't seen
In so many years, it was the Governor smiling
Superciliously. But that smile abruptly vanished
When Dentes slid the shroud open further
And snagged the Governor's sleeve
And dragged him with him, as he was slung into the sea.
The Governor screamed terrified,
And as Dentes dragged the Governor with him.
And they both screamed as they
Continued on into the ice cold water.
As Dentes tread water, the Governor ceased screaming
After Dentes held him under long enough for the man to drown.
There a small log floating by that Dentes clung to
As he untied himself, and began swimming away from
Chateu d'IF, Dentes laughed to himself. "Out of my shroud
And into this icier water, I should be even colder.
But I'm getting warmer. Maybe vengeance
On the cruel Governor was burning hot,
And I'm becoming even hotter when I think of
The Attorney General back in Marseille.
Dentes stared across the water. It was too
Gray to see far away from the cliff,
But he headed in that direction anyway.

He reminded himself, "From my years of swimming
In all kinds of weather, I know I will be
Better than where he had been. So, off he went,
Eager to reach even greater freedom.
He was still going strong, when he heard something.
"Is that the flapping of sails?" Then he yelled out eagerly,
"I'm here! "I'm here! I'm . . ." Then he hesitated.
But he was proud being who he was.
"I'm Captain Edmond Dentes, of the merchant ship Pharon,
And I need your help!" "Need help doing what," was asked.
He didn't want say he wanted revenged, so he didn't answer
Until the ship slowly veering away veered away.
"I'll tell you if you bring me aboard."

The ship veered toward him again,
And he was dragged aboard.
The man who obviously the Captain of the ship,
Laughed, "You don't look much like a captain.
That's some ancient uniform. I don't want
Such trash on my ship. I should toss you back
Into the drink." From the tone of his voice,
Dentes knew he didn't mean it, but another
Short and happy looking sailor came to
Dantes' rescue. "Let's not do that Captain.
I'll clean him up, and maybe we can dress him
In the clothes of maybe the tallest man on our ship."
"Okay, but first let's see what he knows
About piloting a ship. That will tell us if is really
A captain "Where are we, Captain Edmond Dentes,
And where should we headed, and how
Will you get us there?" After Dentes
Was dressed in old but dry clothes,
And after taking a deep grateful breath,
He directed, "We are off the cursed Isle' de IF. . ."
The Captain interrupted, "You look like you
Know it well," and he smiled.
Dentes stood even taller, and also smiled,
And began giving answers to all of the ships crew.

To all of the Captain's questions. After a while,
The Captain seemed to grow more and more
Amazed. "Well, well Captain, here, take the wheel."
Dentes did so, and headed further away from
His former prison, and toward home . . .
Where he would get his wonderful revenge.
Dentes continued his captaining,
Until his hunger weakened him so much
That begged to be fed. "Oh my yes"
Said the Captain, and the more I feed you, the more
You will relieve me of my work."
Dentes ate eagerly, and leaning with his back
The bulkhead, he quickly fell asleep.

And so commenced Captain Dentes' captaincy.
After many day, he directed the ship into
And out of the port on an out of the way island,
Where they met another ship late at night
And exchanged goods. Then Dentes
Knew for certain that his was on a pirate ship,
Which suited Dentes just fine,
He would need his share of the take
To finance his search and obtaining
Of the treasure that his farther, the Priest,
Had promised him. It had been
It had been a long time since Dentes had been this happy.
"Oh Father Abbe, hear my praise," he called out,
As I look up at the heaven at night, I see you smiling down
On me. Please be with me in all my journeys, and help me
See both sides of every challenge, and do what you would do.
And then I will know it is the right thing to do."

And one of those challenges is to head toward Monte Cristo.
When the Captain asked him why, he answered
Reassuringly, "We are short on food, and I know this island
To have wild goats, and I'm an excellent shot, and I'm
Even a good enough to chop one up. The Captain laughed
His easy laugh, and agreed. Then Dentes' rescuer. Whose name

Was Jacopo, piped up, "And I will go with him, Captain,
To help with the heavy load. The Captain lazily nodded,
And Dentes also agreed. And then, another part of his plan
Was forming in his mind. So, the next morning,
He and Jacopo trudged up the twisting trail
To Mount Monte Cristo. "Why are we passing
So many goats?" Asked Jacopo "Too small."
Dentes answered. "Our crew hasn't eaten meat
In weeks." And so on they went up what was
Apparently a goat trail, until the going got so rough,
They had to stop and rest. "Thank goodness,"
Jacopo panted, you might be a mountain climber,
But I'm just an out of shape sailor." Dentes looked
Over at his new friend, who was obviously not
Out of shape, and smiling in a now confidential manner
That Jacopo obviously hadn't expected, Dentes said,
"Jacopo, you are my friend, and can I trust you?"
When Dentes thought the word friend, he grimaced briefly,
Remembering that friend, Fernand, who hadn't been
A true friend. But Jacopo, not knowing what Dentes thinking,
Looked honored and eagerly said, "Yes, sir! Yes, sir!"
"Good, my new friend, I am going to tell you
A secret that you must never share with anyone else"
Jacopo leaned forward as Dentes pulled out the cloth bag
Upon which was drawn the location of Father Abbe's treasure.
"Somewhere in a cave up this mountain, is hidden
An unbelievably large treasure, that you and I
Are going to uncover what will make me one of the
Richest men In the world." And Jacopo now looked
On Dentes with such respect that he seemed to find this easy
To believe, and he said so as Dentes studied the map,
And added it to the other half of the map in his head,
And then decided, "It shouldn't be too far up the mountain.
Let's hurry. The Captain will be wanting his meat."
Then, it wasn't too long before they came to
A small crack in the cliff wall where it appeared that someone
Had tried to disguise a larger crack, which could possibly
Be an entrance into a cave. It didn't take long before

They were able make their way into a dark cave.
There was just enough light for them to see a pile of dirt.
For a moment, Dentes felt disappointed,
But he quickly reassured himself that his Father
Wouldn't have misled him. "Thank you again, Father."
Then he quickly dug aside the caked dirt, to uncover a large
Leather trunk, and dragged it out into the sunlight.
It took a while to pry it open with his knife,
But what they discovered so amazed them
That he and Jacopo could only gasp and stare.
Inside the trunk were three compartments.
The two outer compartment were was piled deep
With enough shining gold coins to purchase
A whole town. The middle compartment
Was filled with diamonds, emeralds, and rubies
That must have been worth far more than the gold.
"Holy Mother of Christ!" gushed Jacopo
I'm messing my pants!" Dentes managed
To hold in his awe by laughing at Jacopo,
"My friend, that doesn't sound so reverent."
"Sorry, Captain, but I mean I'm really impressed!"
"Me too, friend, but I'm filing my bag, not my pants,
With some of these jewels, enough to finance
The next stage of our buying the world."
He did so, and they dragged the trunk
Back into the cave, packed it over with dirt,
And did their best to hide the entrance
To the cave with stones. They were
So excited that Dentes missed shooting
Three goats, but the Captain and crew
We too hungry to ask any questions,
And quickly took to cooking the goats.
Dentes also ate, but his thoughts
Of what he was going to do with
His treasure was happily filling his belly.

The Captain was also happy to fill his belly,
And that, plus his growing comfort

73

In Dentes' decisions, readily agreed
To Dentes's suggestion that their ship
Should make its next dock at Marseille
"Fine with me," the Captain agreed.
"My men have done all that we required
Of them, so a few rounds at the pub
Would be appreciated "Right, sir," Dentes agreed,
"And Jacopo and I have a few errands to run,
And you will be pleasantly surprise at us
When we return." The Captain said nothing,
Already hustling men off ship.
"Surprise? Jacopo asked. "Yes you will
Like it too." Their first stop was a barber shop,
Where both of them were cleanly shaved
And trimmed, and compared to their previous
Appearance they almost sparkled.
Then they were off to purchase new clothes.
Dentes had himself dressed even better
Than the finest French gentleman,
And Jacopo only a little less so.
Then, before leaving the clothing store,
Dentes bought what was obviously
The garb of a priest. Jacopo laughed,
"Sir, though you now have the priest's jewels,
You are obviously not a priest."
"No, and considering what I plan
To do with this garb, I'm more like the Devil."

Now, dressed his clerical garb, while Jacopo
Waited outside, Dentes entered a small Inn
And introduced himself to the owner,
Caderousse, who bowed deeply when Dentes
Named himself as Father Abbe Faria,
Of Rome. "Masseur Caderousse, I am here
To inquire about the family and friends
Of a prisoner of Chateu d'IF whose interment
I attended. With his dying breath,
He recommended you as one who

74

Might have such information."
Caderousse blanched, Dentes guessed
Because he had information he
Didn't want to divulge. "Yes, yes," he finally
Sighed I have things to tell you
That still saddens and shames me,
Shames me because I was drunk
During most of what happened."
"I will listen, and not judge you,
Good sir" Dentes whispered.
And so Caderousse told Dentes
About Danglars, Fernand, and even
Made reference to Prosecutor Gerad de
Villeford. "Ah, my obvious enemy, Danglars,
And my so called fried, Fernand, and
My friendly prosecutor, Gerad," Dentes sighed.
"Here's where my revenge begins."
It seems that Danglars had so cleverly
Mismanaged Masseur Murrel's shipments
That the owner lost money while Danglars
Had had acquired enough money
To buy a small mansion. Then, Fernand's story
Was more complicated. He had married
And tried to comfort the bereaved Mercedes.
Then he tried to impress her by joining Napoleon's
Army, first as a lieutenant, and then
He so charmed Napoleon that he rose
To a Colonel and aid to Napoleon.
And being even more devious, when
Napoleon was defeated, he convinced
The King of France's officers that he was spying
On Napoleon. He must been very convincing
For, with the money had been stealing from Napoleon's
Fallen enemies, he was awarded with enough money
To purchase a large mansion. And then since he was
Already Count, he was able to ensconced his Lady Mercedes
In his new regal mansion. But Mercedes, although her beauty
And lady-like demeanor fitted such a mansion,

Caderorusse believed that she was not happy.
But she did spend most of her time loving
And educating her child. Fernand was so angered
At his wife's coldness to him that
He spent most of his time away from her,
Either gambling, or seeing other women.
Dentes took in this information with mixed feelings,
Sad that Mercedes was unhappy, but glad
That Fernand was even unhappier,
Though as devious as Fernand was,
He probably didn't lose any money.
Now Dentes had what he had come for,
Enough information to guide him in his search
For revenge. He thanked the now relieved Caderousse
And left to go with Jacopo to go back to the ship.
When they got there, the crew heard
The Captain gasping, and rushed onto
The deck to also gape at their two splendidly garbed
Shipmates. The Captain finally recovered,
And smiled knowingly. "Well, fine gentlemen,
I see your are prepared to elegantly
Seek revenge on someones who
Probably doesn't suspect what's
Going to happen to him. So, my
Clever friend, how can I help?
Is there someone you want murdered?"
The Captain asked, smiling. "No," Dentes answered.
"Murder would be too quick, and therefore
Almost painless. I want to hurt my someones
Where it hurts much more that. I want
To rob them of their lives by robbing them
Of their wealth. "Even better," said the Captain.
And how else can I help you?" "This way, Captain.
Jacopo and I will buy our way off your ship,
And then be on our happy way."
The Captain paused briefly, looking somewhat unhappy,
But then sighed. "As you wish, but I do hope
You remember me if you need further service."

"Indeed, friend Captain, your special kind
Of service will be needed again."

"Jacopo, we need a small one-mast boat.
So, let's look along the dock here to see
What we can find. Ah, there's one!
It looks refinished, and there's the owner
Just finishing up" The two, obvious gentlemen,
Approach the man and asked, "My good man,
I would like rent your fine boat overnight."
The owner, obviously impressed by these
Fine gentleman, was reluctant to refuse.
"Sir, I have just repaired my boat,
And I need to get to fishing. My family
Needs the food that I can buy with fish sales"
Dentes pulled out his bag of coins
And began dropping them from one hand
To the other. The owner's eyes popped open.
Then Dentes, smiling, said, "I believe
That this should feed your family
While we are gone. The owner shook his head, "Yes,"
And passed the docking rope to Dentes.
"Thank you, my good man, I have
A few errands to run first, and I will be
Back this afternoon." "Jacopo, we will need
To get ourselves to a solid bank,
So rent a carriage and have it standing by this dock
To await our return tomorrow. "Very good,
And as always, sir." agreed Jacopo.
"And now, let us put on our old sailor
Outfits to protect these fancy clothes."
They did all that, and were soon at sea,
Heading toward the Isle of Monte Cristo.
The sea was calm, so they got there quickly,
And since they knew the way to the cave,
That climb took little time also.
That night, they settle into blankets
Outside the cave. As he lay there,

Gazing at the stars, Dentes couldn't help
Being gloriously happy. "Oh, Father Abbe,
Thank you for my freedom and our treasure. . .
And he started to talk about revenge,
But he then recalled the boat owner
And how good he felt over-paying him
For the rental of his boat. So, he ended
His prayer of thanks by merely
Smiling at the open, star-lit sky.

ACT III

SCENE I: THE REVENGE BEGINS

The next day, all went as planned.
They loaded the coins and jewels into leather bags
That they had purchased and placed them
Them into the carriage that was waiting by the dock.
While inside the carriage, he and Jacopo
Redressed in the rather plain but
Serious look clothes of British businessmen.
"For this adventure, Jacopo, address me
As Lord Wilmore, of London, here in France
To purchase property as investments"
Jacopo merely smiled, loving the charades.
The carriage took them to a rather formal
And very impressive bank. Dentes was
Equally impressive when appeared inside the bank.
A bank teller, on seeing this impressive customer,
Instantly called out for the bank manager,
Who bowed, and asked, "How may I serve you,
My good sir" Dentes, looking serious, stated,
"Sir, I need to be assured that your bank
Can keep safe a chest that contains
Vital document I will need for my business
Here in Marseille. Have I come to the right bank?"
With more bowing, the bank manager insisted,
"Let me show you our vault, sir," and he led
Denise to the back of the bank,
And after going through many locks,
Showed Dentes the interior of the vault.
"And we have around the clock guards
Who will make your business chest even safer."
With all the show, Denise felt very reassured
That his business materials would be safe
And reasonably available for his business dealings.
So, he had the bank manager, who needed

A rather large clerk to help him
Carry the chest into the vault.
"Rather heavy for paper documents,"
He whispered to himself. Then Dentes
And Jacopo carried the many sacks of coins
And jewels and placed them in the chest.
While the bank manager was outside the vault.
"And safe from the bank manager's hearing too,
He told Jacopo. "Next, Jacopo, we'll need
A comfortable place to stay. You know Marseille,
Direct the driver to an inn that is not too ritzy
For business men," The inn keeper of the inn
That Jacopo chose was all too eager
To accommodate this two serious looking
But wealthy looking gentlemen. "A plush room
For each of you gentlemen, and we also serve meals
In your rooms." Jacopo laughed, "Just like on the ship,
Right sir?" Dentes further elaborated.
"But you didn't have to give extra coins on the ship."

But, before going up to their room,
They returned to the clothing store.
The store manager greeting them warming,
"Glad you're back, but not to be too intrusive,
I wonder why I've sold you so many suits."
Dentes had told Jacopo what to say.
"No mystery, sir, we're actors,
And need many different costumes
For or many Part." "Then I'm glad
I have the best costumes in Marseille."
So Dentes bought as many different
Costumes as he thought they might need.

Then they went back to the inn, where Dentes
Taught Jacopo how to speak with a British accent,
And how to project his voice loudly
As if he was speaking to the back on the auditorium.
Then Dentes left Jacopo to practice,

While he, dressed again as Father Abbe,
To visit a gravestone sculptor.
He addressed the owner of the shop seriously,
"My good sir, I am Father Abbe Faria
With a sacred charge from Rome.
I want you to carve the most artistically
Beautiful gravestone you have ever carved.
It must be about eight feet tall and four feet wide,
And on it must be labeled in Biblical script
These words: Here lies Louis Dentes,
Who died in poverty and grief because his son,
Edmond Dentes, who was wrongly convicted
Of treason and died after being starved and tortured
At Chateau de IT prison." The gravestone sculptor turned
As white as his marble stones. He bowed deeply
And whispered, "Indeed, Father, Indeed!"
The Dentes continued, "And this is equally important,"
He said, as he began shelling out gold coins.
This gravestone must be finished by
Nest Sunday morning. Then, after the parishioners
Have all entered the cathedral, the gravestone
Must be placed where can be seen as the people leave
The cathedral. But, this is also extremely important.
At the bottom of the stone, you will place a plaque
That reads, in bold print. "This is an official
Command from the Vatican. He who attempts
To remove this gravestone will be condemned by God!"
The gravestone sculptor stated just as firmly,
"As God is my judge, it shall be done!
And finally, Dentes spoke the gravestone words.
"Louis Dentes is interred in a pauper's grave
At the rear of this cathedral's lot."
And he continued shelling out coins,
"Have grave diggerss disinter and place it, reverently,
Underneath this gravestone. Understood?"
"Yes, all understood, reverend Father"
Dentes knew that Prosecutors Gerad de Villefort
Regularly attended this cathedral,

So Dentes planned to be waiting across the street,
As the British business man, to see
Veillefort's reaction. He hoped that Villefort
Would be so shocked that he messed his pants.

Next, Dentes when back to the inn
And dressed in worn but clean sailors' garb,
And went to where he knew where he knew
His old ship owner lived. The office
Was certainly not as grand as he remembered it
Nor was it as clean as he remembered it to be.
He went into the offices and asked,
"Sir, are you Monsieur Morrel, the owner
Of the good ship Pharon?" "That is me . . . or was me.
My good ship is no longer good, it is sunk."
Dentes looked shocked. "But it was
Such a fine ship. What happened, sir?"
Morrel became angry, "Easy to answer,
My worthless ship Captain, Danglars,
Mismanaged the ship and crew,
And then he sunk it, even though the sea
Was calm." "Ah yes, I've heard of him."
Dentes remarked, looking disgusted, "But couldn't
You have found a better Captain?"
"I did, but he was falsely accused
And died at Chateu d' IF. "How disgraceful,"
Dentes said. I wish I could ease your pain . . .
But pardon me for not noticing it sooner, sir,
But your office, and you as well,
Do not look so well." Dentes took out the small bag
Of diamonds he had prepared, and dropped
One Monsieur Murrel's desk." "No, no," Monsieur Morrel
Protested. "Yes, yes," Dentes protested, and smiling,
He added, "And I'm sure you noticed,
I'm a lot bigger than you, so there's no point in your protesting.
Then quickly, before Monsieur Murrel could say more,
He exited the office. Outside his need for revenge
Against Danglars began to grip him,

But, once again, the pleasure of helping
The suffering Monsieur Murrel softened him.

Next Dentes and Jacopo went to
A weapons shop. As was his habit now,
He shelled out gold coins one by one,
And as was the reaction of shop keeper,
His eyes grew large, before quickly nodding
Their willingness to do whatever was asked.
The dueling team to be, chose somewhat
Gaudy golden steel swords and matching
But dull practice swords. Then,
In the back lot of the inn, Dentes
And Jacopo, after changing into exercise clothes,
Began dueling, "Sir," Jacopo stated proudly,
"I have to warn you that I was probably
The best swordsman on any pirate ship
On the Mediterranean." To which Dentes replied
By quickly slapping the sword out of
Jacopo's hand. "Remember I was taught
By a military master, and as you can see,
Very well." Back in the inn, they changed
Into the gentleman business men's clothes,
And off they went on the carriage on the
Long ride up to the grass covered
Top of the hills that overlooked Marseille.
Passing several elegant well maintained mansions.
On the road between mansions, the carriage driver
Brought Dentes attention to three disheveled
Men caring swords. Dentes directed the driver
To drive off the road so that the men
Would be facing Dentes when he stepped
Out of the carriage. Apparently they were
Taken aback by Dentes' size. There attitude
Changed from aggressive to apologetic.
"Sir, were just out of work ex-soldiers
Who need money to feed our families
Please sir, we'll only rob you of a few coins."

Dentes quickly slapped the swords
Out of their hands, and, in surprise,
They fell to the ground. "Please sir," one of them begged,
Don't kill us." Kill you?" Dentes laughed, "I'm going
To hire you. So quickly, climb up top of the carriage
And make yourselves comfortable. And, to the driver,
He stated "Let's get started again." When Dentes got back
Into the carriage, Jacopo laughed, "And that was
My vicious master, terrorizing the giant enemy again."
Well, they were rather large," Dentes quipped.
The next mansion they came to was indeed large,
Perhaps larger than all the others, but it was
Anything but well maintained. They turned into
The driveway, and stopped when they came to
A rather sad looking man, sitting a rock wall.
Stepping out of the carriage, Dentes asked,
"My good sir, can you direct men me
To the owner of this . . . mansion?
The man grinned a sad grin, "Your hesitation
Tells me you recognize it is no longer a mansion."
And yes, I can direct you to the owner.
You're looking at him." Dentes smiled sympathetically,
"Well, perhaps I can help you have a happier smile.
I would like to buy your sad mansion,
And make it and you happy again.
The owner looked disbelieving. "Buy why
Would want to buy this dump?" "Because I can."
And he pulled out a very large bag of diamonds,
And began dropping one after the other
Into his open hand. The owner, first looked
Disbelieving, and then appreciative. "It's yours, sir,
And I'll be glad to get rid of it." Dentes
Continued dropping diamonds, "On the contrary,
Sir, I don't want you to rid yourself of the mansion,
I want to hire you to repair your mansion,
And make it as elegant as I'm sure it once was.
I'm sure, seeing your sadness in its disrepair,
You must have had pride in it. I want you

To repair your pride." "Sir, you are not only generous,
You are perceptive. It was once, I say, magnificent.
But unwise investments, and . . . the death of my **wife**,
Made me unable to continue its maintenance.
But, inspired by you, I will rise again, sir.
And by the way, sir, who are you, and why
Are you doing this?" "I am Lord Wilmore
Of the Wilmore Company of London,
And I am here to do rich business with Marseille"
"A plum waiting to be plucked." "I see," laughed
The owner. Well good plucking!" Once again,
Dentes began dropping diamonds. "And is it
True that you had staff that you had to let go,
And you would like to hire back?"
"They would be happy and grateful."
"Then I want you to hire those staff members
And all the workers you will need to return
Your mansion to it former magnificence, or even better
Than it's former state . . . in six months.
The owner, who named himself Rene Paellase,
Paused only briefly, and stated, "It will be done,
Lord Wilmore! "One other thing, and this also
Important. I want you to hire only those people
Who are impoverished. And have them live
In good houses on the back of the property,
Where they can do subsistence farming
To feed themselves and their families.
But they will also be paid, of course.
Rene seemed about to drop to his knees.
But caught himself and nodded respectfully.
"Oh Rene, don't look so worshipful.
This is what my company does to make
Our customers believe we are so benevolent
We couldn't possible cheat them."
Rene shook his head, indicating that he believed
Lord Wilmore couldn't possibly be so devious.
Back it the carriage, Jacopo couldn't help saying
"Dentes, there was never pirate who was

85

As much of a con man as you. Having done instructing
Rene, Dentes had new a problem, one that
He shared with Jacopo. "I have been exhilarated
In making all the preparations for encountering
My enemies, Now I'm faced with encountering boredom.
Although you and I practice swordplay, and I
Will coach you on your various accents,
But other than risking disturbing Rene
By too often visiting the construction
Of my new mansion, I have nothing to do."
Jacopo laughed, "Yeah, me too. Back when
I was a sailor, I at least I was able to visit pubs
To keep busy. Oh, poor me. But now, like you,
I've stopped drinking, so I'm bored nuts."
"And like me, I'm sure you don't want to be drunk
When we're having fun with my enemies"
"Oh one more thing, Jacopo, remember we're friends,
So I will still feel better if, when we're alone,
You call me Dentes, and only when we're impressing
The Marseille snobbery, must you call me sir,
Or Count of Monte Cristo. Then Jacopo chimed in,
"Or how about, Your High Horse! Your Majesty."
"Good, you're not so dumb after all." laughed Dentes.

"Jacopo, here's your new task. Put on your Count of Monte's
Dress, and, very respectful, ask Monsieur Murrel
If he feels well enough to attend the Count's
Opening his new estate. If he does feel well enough
Then have our tailor come and fit him regally,
To come to the estates' opening." "This will
Make me happy too, Dentes." Jacopo said.

Then Dentes went to meet Rene, this time
Dressed as the Count. Rene's mouth dropped open
When he saw Dentes in his regal dress.
"Is this the real you, sir?" he gasped.
"The real me, Rene. Sorry for the deception.
It was necessary for my grand plan,

Which I'll tell you about later. How's the work going?"
"Let me show you." Then Rene took him
On a long tour of the estate. "My Heavens, Rene,
I couldn't be more impressed. Now if you'll
Just make the weather perfect for our opening."
"I'm sorry, that's beyond me, Count."
"Well then, let me see if I can conjure up some
Of my Count of Monte Cristo magic.
It goes like this: the Angry March's wild rain
Brings forth April's barely moist flowers
So when June arrives they'll be no rain,
And our estate opening will be as dry as a desert Seine."
Once again Rene marveled, "Is there anything,
Sir, that you can't do?" Dentes shook his head
Dismissing the compliment, but then muttered
To himself, "There is one thing that I must
Be able to do, be able to damage my enemies,
And then let them know who has done this to them,
Only after my clever damaging is done."

Dentes and Jacopo spent the next few months
Practicing sword fighting and accent training,
And it was with relief that they finally arrived
At the renewed mansion, but this time dressed elaborately
As the Count of Monte Cristo and his aid. Their carriage driver,
Whose name was Jacque, bowed and thanked Dentes
Profusely. "You are the most generous master in the world.
I am not only dressed in you mansion's uniform,
I am the driver of what must be to the world's
Most magnificent carriage. I am so proud
To be your driver, and living at the mansion,
I will always be ready to serve you!"
Dentes responded, "And you are entirely deserving,
Putting up with Jacopo and me all this time,
And never complaining. You have profound patience."
Jacque bowed again and finished unloading
The baggage and carried it into the mansion.

Then Rene came running from the mansion,
Then stopped so suddenly, he almost fell on his face."
"But . . . who are you?" Dentes laughed, apologized,
I felt I had to deceive you, but now I confess,
I am Edmond Dentes, the Count of Monte Cristo,
But do not yet use my given name, please."
Rene recovered quickly and bowed deeply.
"I am sure, sir, you had good reasons.
But let me show you your new mansion.
Ah yes, the mansion of the Count of Monte Cristo.
You will see as we pass through the long
Tree line pathway, we are approaching
The expansive courtyard. Then, as you requested,
I have placed on the left side of the entrance
A high balcony, and on the lower right side,
The platform for the orchestra.
And then there is the staircase leading
Up to that magnificent front door, with its
Small window from which you can see
All of the courtyard. Then, as you requested,
Behind the mansion, are the vegetable gardens,
The pastures, and the homes of the farm families.
None of your employees will ever go hungry.
Nor will I, of course. And you can see
That I have already started to regain my weight."
"More than regained," Dentes laughed.
And I also hope you are happy. You have earned it."
"Positively gleeful, my gracious Count of Monte Cristo."

ACT IV

SCENE I: THE REVENGE IS NOT QUITE WHAT WAS EXPECTED

"The glorious scene is being set, my friend, Jacopo,"
Dentes bellowed. First you will appear on the left balcony,
And in your practiced Parisian French, you will bellow,
"May I have your attention, gracious citizens of Marseille.
Let me introduce you to the Count of Monte Cristo!"
And I will stand forth from the massive brass door
Of my mansion, and, spreading up my arms, I will shout,
I am so glad you have accepted my invitation,
And that I will at last get a chance to make new friends,"
And then with a somewhat hushed voice,
And looking forth to find Fernand, I will say,
And one or two old friends as well. Then I will stand there,
A moment, and let them stare in amazement
At my tall, slender, muscular body, arrayed
In the most outlandishly dazzling stage costume
That we have in our closet. What do you think, Jacopo?"
"I think you are the greatest ham that ever
Strutted on a Paris state. I bow down to you!"
"Oh you theater critics, you can never appreciate
True theater art." "Yes, boss, but I admit,
Your performance makes me painfully impatient
To get on with the actually theatrical comedy."
"Or tragedy," Dentes mutter to himself.

And that is exactly how the great drama began.
And when Jacopo finished his welcome,
And the small orchestra quieted, the Count
Of Monte Cristo burst upon the scene.
Then the milling audience suddenly stilled and gasped,
And someone could be heard to whisper,
"My heavens, it's a Greek god! Then
That Greek god strolled slowly down the stairs,

89

To mingle with the guests on either side of the isle.
And Jacopo had joined him when Dentes
Casually approach Fernand, Mercedes, and
Their son, Albert. Dentes bowed to Mercedes,
And kissed her hand. Mercedes first stared
A moment at Dentes, and then blushed.
Then Jacopo also bowed and kissed Mercedes' hand.
Then Dentes became more formal, and standing
Stiffly and much taller than Fernand,
Addressed him, asking, "I feel that we have met
Before, could that be so?" Fernand had trouble
Responding a moment, but managed to whisper,
"No . . . I don't believe so." Then Dentes
Addressed the son. "Oh my, now this is a son
To be proud of. I would guess fifteen or so years,
And already taller than your father.
At the same time Mercedes beamed and
Fernand scowled, and Albert beamed even
Broader than his mother. Then he spoke
Firmly. "I thank your great Count. Your praise,
Is far more than I deserve." "Nonsense,
Nonsense," Then he stepped aside
To let Jacopo firmly shake the young man's hand.
Then Jacopo turned to Fernand, and merely stared.

Then Dentes and Jacopo moved on to further greet
The eager guests, until they reached the former
Crown Prosecutor, Gerad de Villefort.
Gerad was at first puzzled, but then he looked concerned.
"Count, you look as though you know me,
But I don't believe I know you" "Must have been
Another life," Dentes remarked casually. Perhaps
It will come to us later." The Gerard looked even
More concerned, and hearing this remark,
He quickly looked away. Jacopo lifted his
Stern stare for Gerad, and grinned at Dentes.
Muttering, "You got him worried, boss."
"Yes indeed, old friend, yes indeed!"

And then they rushed to meet Pierre Murrel,
The former boat owner, who was looking well
And also well dressed. "Who is this young man,
So strong and well dressed.?" "Your greatest and most
Appreciative admirer," "My thanks, but let us
Find your old boat captain, and let him know we
Have some questions to ask him. But Danglars
Wouldn't wait. He quickly hurried away,
And Dentes laughed and patted each other
On the back. But Dentes wasn't as happy
As he had hoped to be. "Good Father,"
He muttered, "I don't seem to have your blessing on this.

But dismissing this thought, Dentes returned
To the staircase, and loudly addressed the milling'
Guests. "Monsieurs and Mademoiselles,
I see that you are enjoying the food you are eating.
Let me tell you where the this food is coming from.
My friend, Jacopo and I were simple sailors,
Sailing all over the world, and, of course,
As healthy young sailors sampling exotic foods.
We also sampled what we could buy in one port
And sell in the next port for a great profit,
Until, eventually we became so successful,
We were able to purchase our own ship.
And then we continued trading so successfully,
We came back to Marseille, two rich almost
Old sailors able to buy this fine mansion
And feast you fine guests." Then someone asked,
Somewhat sheepishly, "And put us all out
Of business?" "Not to worry, sir, we're tired
Of making money, and just want to spend it.
Then there was a collective sigh of relief
From the now laughing guests.

The next day, Rene brought an apologetic
Young Albert to see Dentes. "I'm sorry
If I'm intruding, I'll come back later

If you'd like." "No, no, son, what's on your mind?"
"Well, sir, I know that you've been everywhere,
So please tell me about Rome. My friend and I
Are going to the festival there, and I don't
Want to do anything to embarrass my Mother."
Dentes laughed, "Very kind of you, son,
But what I have to tell you is obvious.
Don't drink too much, and choose girls carefully."
"Not to worry about the drinking. I'm like you,
I don't drink, but I guess I'll have to learn
About girls." Dentes laughed again, "Well,
Don't learn too rapidly." After Alfred left,
Jacopo said to Dentes "You sounded rather happy
In telling your son what to do." "Yes, I know,
I guess this must mean that I would like
To have a son like Albert. He's a fine young lad.
But I have just thought of a plan to see
How my son can prove himself in a challenging
Situation. Hire a boat to take us to Rome,
And alert our friends, the pirates, to meet us there."

Once in Rome, Dentes had no time finding
Albert in the gaily milling crowd in the
Roman festival, but he made Albert didn't see him.
Then, what happened next, went just
As Dentes planned it. A masked, but obviously
Pretty young girl, beckoned Albert down
A dark alley, and Albert eagerly followed.
Then, also as Dentes had planned,
Albert was jumped and masked by
Dantes' masked pirate friends, who dragged
Albert further down the ally and pushed
Down on a curb. Albert struggled strongly
At first, but stopped, but sat up straight.
"Well, what have we got here?" the pirate chief smirked.
"Some Mommy's spoiled rich kid just waiting to tell us
Where is Mommy lives so she can send
Us his ransom money?" Dentes was surprised

92

And also impressed that Albert merely laughed,
"Forget it, you cowards too frighten to face me
Without masks. I'll telling you nothing."
"Oh yeah, how's your Mommy going to feel
When we send her your pretty head?'
"I can't believe you're that stupid. You don't know
Where my Mother lives, and you are not
Going to kill the boy who will earn you your ransom."
Dentes was enjoying the show that Albert
Was putting on, but it was time to end it.
He motioned the pirates to re-mask themselves,
And then he pulled forth his sword and
Whirled it about. Then the pirate chief
Shouted out, "Oh Jesus and Mary, It's the
Count of Monte Cristo! He's the greatest
Swordsman in the world. Run for your life!"
The pirates disappeared, then Dentes removed
Albert's mask, stood him up and hugged him.
Albert looked both relieved and ashamed.
"I'm such a fool. I did just what you told
Me not to do. Please don't tell my Mother."
"Not to worry. Anyway, I don't know where
Your Mother lives, someplace here in Rome,
I believe?" The Dentes and Albert both laughed,
And Jacopo nudged Dentes, "Enough hugging,
Father. "But one can wish, friend,
One can wish."

SCENE II: FAREWELL, DANGLARS

Caderousse had told Dentes that Dangler did
A lot of drinking, so he and Jacopo and the pirates
Met Danglar as he came stumbling out of
A dock-side pub. They quickly dragged him
Into a side ally and shoved him down on a curb.
"Hey!" he shouted, "What's this? I got no money.

93

Anyway, I'm a ship captain. You can trust me.
I can get your money to you later." Dentes laughed,
"I learned from Monsieur Murrel just how
Much you can be trusted. By the way,
Monsieur Murrel sends his greetings,
And wishes you a short, sad voyage.
And now I want you to recognize
Who will be sending you on your voyage.
I am your old, short-lived captain Edmond
Dentes, otherwise known as the Count
Of Monte Cristo. And since you are such
An able captain yourself, or at least as crafty
As these pirate friends of mine, they are
To set you far out to sea in a small
Row boat, and leave you with a pint of wine,
And no water, and no paddles, so you
Will have to hand paddle yourself until
You die of thirst or jump overboard
And drown yourself. Then I hope you
Remember your captain-to-be, Edmond
Dentes, but you can be sure he won't be
Thinking of you. Take him away my good
Friends" And then he turned his back
On the begging Danglars . . But as
He walked away with Jacopo, he muttered,
"I hate myself for thinking this,
But I almost feel sorry for him.

SCENE III: FAREWELL, GERAD

Dentes and Jacopo were waiting in his carriage
As Gerad came out of his bank. He had
A pleased expression on his face as he
Studied his bank statement. The expression
Became startled as two gendarmes grabbed
Him by his arms, saying, "Are you Gerad de

Villefort?" "What is this? Take your hands off me!"
Ignoring Gerad's protest, the gendarmes
Shoved him into an iron wagon, and
Drove off with him. Dentes and Jacopo
Followed to the Crow Prosecutor's office,
And waited outside, but where they
The conversation in the office.
A young but firm voice said,
"You are Gerad de Villefort, formerly
Of this office?" Gerad was growing more angry,
"In fact, I am. Now tell me why you have
Dragged me here?" "Be quiet, Gerad, I will
Ask the questions. And are you the former
Deputy Crown Prosecutor, who arrested
And an innocent young sailor named
Edmond Dentes and sentenced him
To be confined and to die at Chateu d'IF?"
Now Gerad was becoming worried,
"But he was guilty, . . ." "He was not!
And now you will be the one to be
Confined and to die at Chateu d'IF.
The Prosecutor's voice became even
Sterner, "Gendarmes, take this man
To the boat in which he will be taken
To his prison" Gerad was not becoming
Obviously frightened, but angry,
"You can't do this! Don't you know who
I am!" "I do indeed," said the Prosecutor,
Sounding satisfied, "That is why the Count of
Monte Cristo so kindly informed me
Of your influence over some people
Of wealth, and why I must send you
Immediately to your prison so you
Can't buy your way out of your just
Imprisonment. Take him away, gendarmes!"
Dentes and Jacopo waiting by the boat
"Gendarmes, please wait. I have something
To say to your prisoner." With a smile

On his face, Dentes asked quietly,
"Do you recognize me, former Assistant
Deputy Prosecutor?" "Yes, you're the Count."
"Yes, see now a young sailor, frightened
And bewildered, a young sailor named
Edmond Dentes. Gerad now lost his anger,
And became obviously frightened,
And he collapsed, begging, "No! No!
Please don't do this!" "Yes, I will do this
Happily, but I will grant you one last request.
My bride-to-be, Mercedes knew what
Had happened to me. So, I will let your
Wife know what has happened to you.
And since I am not so unfeeling as you were,
`She can keep your estate. But I wonder
How concerned about you. Gendarmes, do your
Job" Smiling, perhaps because they
Appreciated what was happening, as the
Iron gate in the boat slammed shut,
And the boat sailed off to Chateu d'IF.

Destes stood a moment on the dock,
And wistfully whispered to Jacopo,
"Once again, Father Abbe is asking me
To carefully examine my feelings, and
I'm disparately trying not to." "Ah,
The curse of the Holy Father," said
Jacopo, "So maybe you need to confess."

SCENE IV; FAREWELL, FENAND

Dentes and Jacopo are sword fighting o
T he estate front lawn, and Dentes
Comments, it's a good thing I'm being
Careful with my sharp blade or
I could cut your head off"

"And if I were your old friend Fernand,
You would cut my head off, yes?"
"That thought occurred to me lately,
But . . . What's this?" Young Albert,
Obviously upset, jumped out of his carriage,
Shouting, "Please. Count, you must come
To my home. My father is drunk, and
He's swinging his sword about, shouting
At my Mother, calling her a whore. Please
Come!" Dentes and Jacopo sheaved their
Swords, jumped into Albert's carriage,
And away went. At the Fernand mansion,
It was as Albert had said. Albert's Mother
Was huddled among her servants and
One of her guards, who was fending off
Fernand's sword with his own. Dentes
Quickly intervened, "Fernand, what are
You doing? This is your wife you are
Threatening, and this is your son who
You are upsetting. Please, back off,
And put down your sword." Fernand
Swung his sword even wilder, and
Shouted, "Well, here comes the whore
Master to claim his reward. And what
Do you mean, My son? Look at him.
Don't you see he doesn't look like me,
He looks like his true father, the noble
Count of Monte Cristo. Or in other word,
My old friend, Edmond Dentes."
Then, the whole scene seemed to freeze.
Dentes still his sword right before him,
Mercedes' face had lit up, Albert looked
Back and forth between Fernand and Dentes,
And Jacopo's expression said that
He knew it all along. But then the
Frozen scene broke, and Fernand sighed,
"Well, let truth control this final scene.
And with this, he thrust his sword

Toward Dentes' chest. The move was
Too quick for Dentes to move aside his
Own sword, and when Fernand lunged
Toward Dentes, Dentes' sword
Pierced Fernand's chest right near
His heart. "Ah ha. Now who's the noble
One?, he gasped, and fell backward,
Pulling Dentes's sword from his bleeding chest.
Dentes was too stunned to move,
But Jacopo wasn't. He quickly shoved
Dentes aside and then pulled Dentes'
Sword from Fernand's wound and
Gave it a great heave, where it could be
Heard sticking in a floating log
Which would bring down the rive
To the sea down below, "Where it
Will return to where my friend's journey
Began so long ago. And I also believe
That the revenge blood has been wiped
Clean from my friend, Denten's heart.
Then Jacopo grinned, as he looked
Over at his friend's family. "And now
We can live happily ever after!" That
Happy remark unfroze all t he the others,
Although it did take Jacopo to bring
The scene to an end. He dragged
Dentes to Mercedes, and flung Dentes
Eagar arms about her, and then he also
Shoved Albert to wrap his arms about
His parents. Then, finally, he hugged
The happy family himself, saying, Uncle
Jacopo is also a part of this family,
And he can't wait for his nephew, Albert.
To give us some Count of Monte Cristo
Grandkids. And then he whispered,
And for Grandfather Abbe to have
Some grandkids." Then he further whispered,

"And I know you are hearing, me,
Father, so we will all appreciate your blessings."

THE NARRATOR SUMMARIZES THE PLAY

Dear theater audience, I'm sure you recognize this plot. The violated lead character seeks to get revenge on those who have harmed him. Bit when the plot changes him, he begins to have compassion for his persecutors. Shakespeare didn't too often have his characters show compassion, but in this play, compassion seems to be a telling part of the lead character.

So, as Shakespeare might say,
"Vengeance is sweet, but compassion isn't sour,
So, let your vengeance fade away,
And let barrels of sweet fruit fall
From your heart's bower
At the beginning of everyday.

THE HOBBIT

AS TOLD BY SHAKESPEARE

SCENE I: THE NARRATOR BEGINS THE PLAY

Bilbo Baggins is a self-satisfied and self-contained Small Person, not a dwarf, who lives in an equally self-satisfied hobbit village at the foot a moderately high hill that doesn't require much effort to get about for sellers or visitors. At the opening of the play, Bilbo has fixed himself a cup of warm tea, and he is enjoying just thinking about how satisfied he is with his situation: a hobbit doing only what he has to do to get along rather well.

But this is about to change when he hears a knock on his modestly decorated front door. Now, the modest middle aged Hobbit is about to become a great "Burglar" and a rather gifted one at that. Be advised, audience, that Bilbo has the habit of talking aloud to himself, but so quietly that no one else can hear him.

This is another indication of his modesty. He just doesn't want **to** impose on another person's thoughts or conversation.

So, audience, come along with Bilbo Baggins' journey to a greatness that he can't believe is happening.

ACT I

SCENE I: AN UNEXPECTED PARTY

Bilbo was standing outside his cottage door,
Admiring the calm greenery of his neighborhood
When he saw an old man with a staff.
"Good morning," meaning it, for the sun
Was shinning, And his world welcomed him.
"Do you wish me A good morning or are you Just stating
That the **morning is good?**
But I have no time for idle chit chat,
I'm looking for someone to share
An adventure with me and it's
Very difficult to find such a one."
That doesn't sound very good to me at all,
Bilbo muttered to himself as he prepared
To shut his door. The old man blocked him,
Stating, "I know your name. You are Bilbo
Baggins, but I don't think you know my name.
I am Gandalf, sometimes know as
The Wandering Wizard." Bilbo gasped,
"Gandalf! Gandalf! Good gracious me!
Not the wizard who knows all. I didn't know
You were still in business." But the Wizard
Just stood waiting, until Bilbo decided
He had enough adventure this fine morning,
So without trying to close his door again,
He stated politely, "I wish you another
Good day, but do come back again
For some morning tea, and why not tomorrow?"
"Why not today," said Gandalf, as he
Shoved his way past Bilbo, and Bilbo
Could do nothing but race further
Into his home to seek tea. When he returned,
He was greeted by a series of dwarfs,
Who announced themselves as they came

Into Bilbo's soon crowed parlor,
"Dwalin, at your service." "Balin, at your service.
"Bifer, at your service." "Bofor, at your service."
One after another until there were eleven
Of them. Then the largest, but clean shaven
Dwarf entered, Very business like,
And Announced himself As,
"Thorin, Chief Of these dwarfs, at your service!"
To which Bilbo whispered, "Bilbo Baggins,
Also at your service," and hurried to his
Kitchen to fetch more tea-making equipment.
When he returned, Gandalf was saying,
"Now that we're all here" looking at the row
Of thirteen hooded heads, "It's time for a party,
Before our adventure, during which
We will require our host, The Bugler, .
Bilbo Baggins." "Here! Here!" cried twelve
Of the dwarfs, except for Thorin, who seem
Less than enthusiastic. Gandalf smiled avt Thorin,
"I think you will be pleasantly surprised,
By our creative host, Bilbo." Thorin just
Shook his head, but added more enthusiastically,
"We'll see, but first let's see how creative his is
At our feast." Which sent Bilbo off
To his kitchen again frantically preparing
To feed the ravenous dwarfs. And so began
This feast was a mixture of eat, or actually
Gorging, With intermittent singing:

Clip the glasses and crack the plates!
Blunt the knives and bend the forks!
Smash the bottles and burn the cork!
That's what Bilbo Baggins hates!

Bilbo didn't want to hear any more
Of the raucous songs, so he hurried
Back and forth between the parlor
And the kitchens, shutting his ears

To the possibility that any of this destruction
Might be happening. He only consoled
Himself with the thought that this parting
Would end, and he could return to the peace
And quite of his ordinary Hobbit home.
"All Of this," he was muttering to himself, but, on
The other hand, did he see Gandalf smiling
And shaking his gray-bearded head?

But, this time when he returned to his parlor,
All had quieted. Almost in a whisper,
The dwarfs began singing a new song:

Far over the misty mountain cold,
To dangerous deep and caverns old,
We must away ere break of day
To seek the pale enchanted gold.

Then song continued on to elaborate
On the this history of the dwarfs'
Struggle to recover the stolen and lost
Treasures of the ancient dwarf kingdom,
Which was to whole purpose of this gathering
Of new dwarfs, a gathering of obtaining
And also profound longing for what might be
Unobtainable. In reviewing what he though
He was hearing in this singing, Bilbo paused
In his indifference, and almost began
To wish to join this great adventure,
And adventure that was so much more
Exciting and even noble than his
Comfortable stay-at-home Hobbit life.
But then the clutter in his parlor brought
Him back to reality. "I'll just clean up
This mess and bid my disruptive guests
On their adventurous way," he muttered,
"So I can settle back into my comfortable
Hobbit life," Again, Gandalf the Wizard,

Seemed to be reading his thoughts, and
And also muttering, "Nay! Nay! reluctant
Burglar, nay, nay." In spite of his exhaustion,
And a side order of fear, Bilbo managed
To sleep all night without waking.
When he did wake, it was with a start.
He rushed to his parlor, ignore the chaos,
And complained, "They left without me!"
Then he caught himself, and laughed,
"Who am I kidding? I'm glad they left without
Me. Imagine me, "Bilbo Baggins, happy to be
In my well ordered home, dashing off
To be some courageous burglar—
Poppy cock!" But then he sighed,
And considered that fantasy. "Poppy cock!"
He repeated. But, suddenly, Gandalf barged
In"My dear fellow, when are you ever going
To come? I left a message." "What message?"
"Don't you ever dust your mantle?"
"Ever day, all my adult life." "So you must
Have seen the message." Bilbo rushed
To the mantle and quickly read the long
Message, That thanked Bilbo for his
Hospitality, and urged him to meet him and
His fellow dwarfs at The Green Dragon Inn.
"So, you have ten minutes. Gather your gear, And let's go!"
"Gear, what gear" "All the gear you
Will need to do Your famous burglaring!"
So, as it turns Out, Bilbo packed his pack with probably
More than he would ever need—but he forgot
His hat, a walking stick, or any money
That didn't matter To the dwarfs.
They were Already moving off on small horses,
One of which Bilbo mounted, Awkwardly.
Horse riding wasn't something one
Did in Hobbit Land. Soon, however,
They encountered Gandalf mounted on a
Splendid white horse, burdened down

With food, and so Bilbo decided maybe
This adventure wasn't going to be so bad
After all. But the terrain was another thing.
Bilbo had never travel far from Hobbit Land,
So he was both enchanted and concerned
By all the hills of greenery they were passing
Through. Gandalf noticed his Bilbo's awe.
"Beautiful But strange, I admit. I call it
New Zeeland, New because it's every changing, and
Zeeland, Because it's like an awkward Pronouncing child,
Shouting, "Zeewize! Zeewize!
As he prances through the Green Meadows,
Bilbbo was startled that
The usually somber Wizard, Seemed childlike himself.

ACT II

SCENE I: THE ROAST MUTTON

At first they passed through Hobbit Lands,
Wide open fields, where friendly people
Greeted them. Next, the trail led them
Through less friendly lands, with few
People and few houses, and no inns
Just the stone ruins of ancient castles.
This made Bilbo begin reminisce
About his familiar Hobbit Home,
And he soon found himself lagging
Behind the others, who ignored him.
It was nearly night before they
Crossed over an old bridge, and
Since the side of it gave them
Some shelter, Thorin decided the
Would camp for the night. It was
Only then that Bilbo cried out,
"Where is Gandalf!' And sure
Enough, the Wizard was missing!
But that was a mystery that was
Of less interest to the dwarfs,
It was food that was on their
Minds. But, unfortunately, it was
Food that suddenly was not there.
The food-carrying pony bolted,
for no apparent reason, and the
food bag was washed away down
Stream. So, there was little to
Eat that evening. Then Bilbo was
Distracted. "Look, there's a light
Over there! On a hill, with some
Trees on it. It might be worth
Checking on." So, they started too,
But it started to rain. Then Thorin

Ordered, "While we settle in, I think
Our Burglar friend should steal over
There, and let us know what he
Can bring back to us." The others
Caught the pun, and Bilbo wasn't
Gracious as he headed toward the
Light. When he got near the
Flickering light, he saw it was a
Campfire, and seated about
The burning logs were several
Enormous beings, one of whom was
Grumbling about mutton. "I could
Use some raw mutton to cook
Over this fire. But then one of then
Spotted Bilbo, and grabbed at him.
Perhaps Bilbo was so small,
Compared to the monster's hand,
Bilbo slipped away. "Come back
Here, whatever you are, I won't eat
You. You're too small anyway. "I'm
A Hobbit, and I eat sour Hobbit
Food. So, I would give your big
Tummy an ache." "Okay, but since
You were able to sneak up on us,
You must have been able to sneak
Up on something bigger and better
For us to eat, like maybe dwarfs.
"No, never seen any dwarfs," pipped Bilbo,
And scurried back to warn his dwarf
Friends. But, unfortunately, the dwarfs
Had been worrying about Bilbo,
And on seeing them, he shouted,
"Don't come any closer, there
Are monsters here!" "They're
Trolls! Don't let them catch you,
They will eat you!" That made the
Trolls happy. "Yes, we eat thing,
And you look like dwarfs, and

Dwarfs taste even better than
Mutton," said one of the trolls,
As he grabbed for Thorin, who was
Leading the others, and caught him
By the leg, and was about to shove
Him into his mouth. But Bilbo
Grabbed the other leg and pulled,
Shouting, "No, no, that's do
Dwarf. Look, it has no beard."
The droll was considering that,
And that gave Bilbo the opportunity
To practice his alleged burglar skills.
He slipped his hand into the
Troll's pocked, fished around
And came upon what felt like
A large keys. "A key could be
Useful" he muttered, and stuck
The key into his own pocket.
But, just at that moment, Gandalf
Reappeared. He carefully lodged
Himself behind a tree trunk beside
Bilbo. "Good work, burglar. A key
Could be useful. Now watch the
Crafty old Wizard work some
Non-wizard wisdom." He stated
The trolls arguing among themselves,
All That the sun was beginning to
Come up. The trolls were so
Involved in their arguing, it
was too late for them to notice
The first rays of the sunlight
Hitting their skin. Then they
Froze like ice, and were easily
Smashed into dusk before
Bilbo's startled eyes. "Trolls
Are night creatures, and can't
Survive in daylight. Now, Thorin,
Take your non-eaten foot

And lead me and our burglar
Friend to find the entrance
Into the troll's cave. We might
Find something worthwhile in
There." Trolin, did as told,
But he didn't look too thankful.
The follow troll tracks until
They came to a large cave door
Where Gandalf tried various
Incantations on the door, and was
Becoming frustrated, when Bilbo,
Smiling said, "Here, let the Master
Burglar do his non-magic." With that
Witticism, he pulled the key
From his pocket, stuck it in the
Keyhole, and, after a click,
They were able to pry the door
Open. Inside, they found a great
Deal of food, pots filled with
Brass buttons, and smaller pots
Filled with gold coins. But more
Interesting, they found two large
Swords, each of which was taken
By Gandalf and Trolin. Then
Bilbo picked up a dagger, which
In Bilbo's small hand, could act
As a sword. "Let's get away from
The death-smell in this troll cave,"
Said the gasping Kali.

SCENE III: A SHORT REST

And spent the rest of
The day eating by a happy fire.
The next day, they brought their
Their ponies up from back

Down the trail. But before
The continued on their journey,
Gandalf shoved the gold coins
And buttons into a crack
Inside ledge, and cast
Numerous spells over it,
Saying, "We might want them,
Should we ever come back
This way." Bilbo muttered his
Dislike about *ever coming back.*
"Of course we're coming back!"
Or at least he was. The dwarfs
Could go on to their dragon
Cave, but master burglar or not,
Bilbo Baggies of his Hobbit
Home was coming back!

Then they all mounted up and
Headed toward the East. Thorin,
With a slightly annoyed tone,
Asked, "Where did you go to,
And why did you come back?"
"To spy ahead. The road soon
Becomes more dangerous and
Difficult. And I had not gone
Very far when I met a friend from
Rivendale. "Where's that?" Bilbo
Asked. "We will get there in
A couple of days, and as I was
Saying, I met a two of Elrond's people.
They were hurrying away from trolls
That had come down from the
Mountain, and they were frightening
People away from the district, and
Waylaying people. I had a feeling that
I'd better get back with you. Please
Be more careful when you are alone."
Thorin thanked him, but not too

115

Courteously. But Bilbo pipped up,
and very courteously, "Thank you,
Gandalf, great wandering Wizard,"
And all the other dwarfs echoed that.

They continued on their way their
Way the next day. "Is that the
Mountain," asked Bilbo, with wide
Wondering eyes. He had never seen
Anything that big before. "And we
Are supposed to climb it?" "Of
Course not." answered Thorin,
In his usual dismissive tone,
"That is only the beginning of
Misty Mountain, and then we
Have to get to the other side, before
We come to the Lonely Mountain
That we must climb to get to
Smaug and our treasure." Bilbo
Felt his heart sink, and he didn't
Even mind Thorin's tone. In fact,
That commanding tone was
Reassuring to him.

Now Gandalf led the way. "We
Must not miss our road, or we
Will be done for. We need food, and
Rest so we don't miss the proper
Path or we will have to start all
Over again, even if we can."
"That doesn't sound like the
Confident Wizard I thought I
Knew," said Thorin. "Me either,"
Whispered Bilbo, not liking that his
His tone said he was agreeing with
Thorin. Gandalf led on, until they
Came to an upward trail covered

With white stones, large and small,
And one just the right size for
Gandalf's horse to stumble over it
And almost through him off. "Here
We are at last!" he called, and the
Others gathered around him. They
Could see a valley far below,
And as they began slipping and
Sliding down the steep trail,
Bilbo, was murmuring, "If I make
It, I'll stop complaining about
Where they're taking me." But
They did make it down, and
Then he cried out "Hmmm, it
Smells like Elves" And that smell
Was followed by a burst of song-like
Laughter in the trees.

O! What are you doing,
And where are you going?
Your ponies need shoeing!
The river is lowing!
O! tra-la-la-lally!

O! Wh at are you seeking?
And where are you making?
The faggots are reeking,
The bannocks are baking!
O! Trill—lil-lil-lilly
the valley jolly,
ha! ha!

O! Where are you goging
With beards all a-wagging?
No knowing, no knowing
What brings Mister Baggins
And Balin and Dwalin
Down into the valley

in June
ha! ha!

O! Will you be staying,
Or will you be flying?
Your ponies are staying!
To fly would be folly,
To stay would be jolly
And listen and hark
Till the end of t he dark
to our tune
ha! ha!

"I see them," laughed Bilbo,
As the darkness deepened. "I love
Them," he grinned. Then a voice
Broke into Bilbo's thinking,
"Well. Well." said a voice, "Just
Look. Bilbo the Hobbit on a
Pony. Isn't it delicious!"

At last. A tall young man came
Out of the trees and bowed to
Gandalf and Trolin. "Welcome
To the Valley!" he said. "Thank
You," said Trolin, somewhat Gruffly.
But Gandalf was already Off his horse among
The elves Talking merrily with them.
"You'll be going a little out
Of your way in getting
To the house over the water, so
You can stay and eat with us."
The dwarfs were eager to eat,
But Gandalf insisted that they
Hurry on. There would also
Be food in the Last Lonely House,
And when they reached it, its
Door was flung wide open.

Therein was a friendly looking
Elf, who named himself Elrond,
And all gathered round him as
He showed interest in the two
Swords that Gandalf and Thorin
Showed him. "Though you
Bought these from the troll lair,
These are very old and from the High Elves of the
West. This, Thorin, is Orcrisrt, that the
King of Gondolin once wore.
Keep them well!" Then he shifted
His interest. "Now Show me
Your map. Now what is this?
I see moon-letters that
Say Stand by the gray stone
When the thrush knocks and the
The setting sun of the last light
Of Durin's Day will shine upon
The key-hole." "Are there any
More Moon-Letters?" "No, none."
"Then let us go down to the
Water and dance and sing with
The fairies." "And eat too?"
Asked Bilbo. "Yes eat too,"
Asked Dwalin. The next morning,
They road away to the singing
And fare thee wells of the
Happy fairies, with their hearts
Filled with the knowledge of
The road they must travel
Over the the Mountain and
Beyond. His friends were so Happy,
Bilbo said to himself, "Maybe
I can enjoy an adventure After all."

SCENE IV: OVER HILL AND UNDER HILL

The way was peaceful and the slope was gentle for a while after
They left the Last Lonely House,
But gradually they began moving
Along side a boulder-strewn cliff.
Then, Sudden heaven rain began.
"I never knew weather like this my
Homeland," complained Bilbo.
But then the weather grew worse.
Boulders began tumbling off the cliff.
"Watch out for the boulders
Rolling down on Us," warned Bilbo.
"Not rolled, being thrown
By stone giants that are playing
Games against one another.
So, we'd better find some
Way to keep from from being Knocked
Off the ledge." Fili and Kili were sent to find some kind
Of shelter. They came back Quickly, saying that they had
Found a cave that looked usable.
"How deep is the Cave?" asked Thorin
. "Deep enough," Was the quick reply. But when
Everyone got to the cave, it was
Only perhaps twenty yards deep.
The other Dwarfs started Complaining, until
Gandalf hushed Them.
"We will make do until
The stone-gaints stop playing"
As they entered the cave, Fili Looking
Further into the warned, "Anyway, who knows
What lurks Further back in this cave. But no one
Worried about that. Instead, the
The dwarfs talked and talked
And soon talked themselves
To sleep. Bilbo did fall asleep,
To his friends, "What a horrible

Dream. A crack opened up
In the back of the cave, and our
Ponies were being dragged away
Through that crack! And then
The floor opened up, and up
Jumped goblins who dragged me
And six of you dwarfs down
A hole that opening up in the
Floor!" Then he realized that
He wasn't dreaming. "Gandalf!
He cried, and there was a great
Flash and the smell of gunpowder,
And several of the goblins fell
Dead. But it was too late, he
And six dwarfs and Thorin were
n the other side of a stone wall,
Being dragged further down
Toward a red flashing light!
Then the goblins started singing,
and it wasn't a happy song.

Clap! Snap! The black crack!
Grip! Grab! Pinch! Nab!
And down, down into Goblin-Town
You go, my lad!

Clash, crash! Crush, smash!
Hammer and tongs! Knocker and gongs!
Pound, pound, far underground!
H, ho! my lad!

Swish, smash! Whip, crash!
Batter and beat! Yammer and bleat
Work, work! Nor dare to shirk!
While Goblin Quaff, and Goblin laugh!
Round and round far underground
Below my lad!

Then the goblins laughed, and
Shoved Bilbo and the others
In front of a huge fire, and

Dragged the ponies off to
A corner of the room. On the
Other side of the fire was a
Tremendous Goblin with a
Huge head. Surrounding him
Were other goblins armed with
Axes, hammers, swords, and
Any other instruments that
Could kill but probably first
Maim anything they encountered.
"Who are these miserable person?"
The Great Goblin demanded.
"Dwarfs, and this thing," said
One of the goblins, dragging
Bilbo around the fire to the
Foot of the Great Goblin.
"We found this and the rest
Of them sleeping on our
Front Porch." "What do you
Mean by this?" the Great
Goblin demanded, turning to
Thorin. "Up to no good, I'll
Warrant, spying on the private
Business of my people. Thieve,
I should guess, Murderous, friends
Of elves, not likely come by.
What have you got to say for Yourselves"
"Thorin, the dwarf, At your service.
We were sheltering from a storm,
and meant no disrespect to your
Grand Front Porch. With your
Permission, we will be on our
Way." "Um," said the Great
Goblin, "And what are you

Doing up here? And where are
You from, and where are you
Going? In fact, I don't need
Your lies. I already know all
About you, Thorin Okenshield.
But let's have the truth, or
I will prepare something very
Unpleasant for you!" "We are
On a journey to visit relatives,
And no more than that." "From
Your quavering voice, It's
Obvious you are making this up.
So, what are you hiding?"
"And he's lying, he's lying.
Several of our people were struck
By lightening. And when we
Invited these people below,
He didn't explain why he was
Carrying this!" and the goblin
Presented Thorin's swords to
The Great Goblin. On seeing
The sword, the Great Goblin
Roared with rage. "This is
The sword that killed hundreds
Of my people. Murderous!
Smash them, beat them, gash
Them, take them away to them
Away to the dark cave to
Be eaten by the giant snakes!
He was in such rage that he
Jumped of his seat and rushed
At Thorin with his mouth open.
At that moment, the light in
The cave went out, and the
Great fire turned was smothered
By a shower of sparks from
A hole in the ceiling, burning
And scattering the terrified

Goblins. Suddenly a sword
Flashed with its own light and
Swished through the air
and chopped off the Great
Goblin's head. And then
The other goblins pulled
Themselves together to flee
from that swishing sword.
"Follow me quick!" said a
Voice fierce and quite, and
Before Bilbo could realize what
Was happening, a pale light
Was leading them on. "Quicker
And quicker! The torches
Will soon go out!" "Wait a
Minute!" said Dori as he grabbed
Bilbo and thrust him up on
His shoulders, and then they
All went running until they
Were down in the heart of
The mountain. But the fleeing
Goblins must have pulled
Themselves together. "Is that
Them I hear behind
Behind us?" Bilbo asked, as
He bobbed up and down on
Dori. "It must be warned Thorin.
Maybe they know shortcuts,
Or they are just faster than us.
But it does sound like they're
Catching up. Let's try to go
Faster, even though it's getting
Darker" They did, and that
Must have been what caused
Dori's pony to stumble and toss
Bilbo off Dori's shoulders. "Yow,"
Yelled Bilbo, and then "My head!
My head! And he felt himself

Being hurled what seemed like
A cliff, and that was all he knew
Until he woke up still complaining,
"My head! My head!"

SCENE V: RIDDLE IN THE DARK

When Bilbo woke up, it was dark,
So he tried to learn where he was
By feeling around. He was still
Groggy, but these things his Fingers told him,
"I'm Leaning Against a stone wall, if
I crawl alongside the wall,
I seem To to be going downhill.
What's this? It feels like a ring.
I'll try it on my finger. It fits.
Good, but I'd better pocket it
So I won't Lose it. Then he
Started slapping his pockets,
Hoping too find Matches.
No luck, but he did feel his small Dagger.
He slapped it to assure Himself,
"At least I can protect Myself.
Then the blade lit up with
A faint blue light "Great!
Now I won't need matches.
So standing, he trotted along,
Though carefully, when his
His hairy Hobbit foot stepped
Into a puddle of icy cold water.
He withdrew his foot, and peered
Ahead. "It's a small stream that
Leads to a large lake. Then he
Stopped talking to himself
To listen and stare further on
To the others side of the lake.

What he saw startled but
Intrigued him. There, stepping
Into a small boat, was a small
Gray-skinned bony creature
Who was seemingly talking to
Himself. "I be Gollum, and
Who be you? Bilbo nearly jumped
Out of his skin, but managed
To stutter, "I be . . . I mean
Bilbo Baggins, at your service."
"Yes, yes, and tasty bit of Baggins,
I would guess. "No, please, I don't
Want to be eaten. I just want to
Get back to my dwarf friends
So we can continue on our Journey.
Will you help me find
My way out of this cave?"
"No, I won't help you, but you
Might win your way out
Do you like solving riddles?"
"No, but I'll try. You ask first"

What has roots nobody sees,
Is taller than trees,
Up, up it goes
And yet never grows?

"Easy," said Bilbo. "Mountains,
I suppose." "Does it guess easy?"
Gollum, seemingly asking himself,
Not Bilbo "Yours will
Be so easy, I will get it Quickly,
And then mine will be so
Unsolvable, I will get to eat you.

Thirty white horse on a red hill,
First they champ,

Then they stamp,
Then they stand still.

"That was easy," hissed Gollum,
But I have only six." And Bilbo
Whispered to himself, "But they're
Mighty big, so I don't want you
Eating me." Then Gollum
Was grinning when he asked his
Second question.

Voiceless it cries,
Wingless flutters,
Toothless bites,
Mouthless mutters.

"Wind, wind of course," Answered Bilbo.
"Now I'll bet you will have
Trouble with this one, living
In this cave like you do.

An eye in a blue face
Saw an eye in a green face
That eye is like to his eye
Said the first eye,
But in low place
Not in high place.

But Gollum answered it quickly,
"Reminds me of my Grannie's
Place. Sun in the daisies it means,
But I don't eat daisies."

So Bilbo said to himself, "He likes
Eating too much, so let me try
Something more unpleasant.

It cannot be seen, cannot be felt,
Cannot be heard, cannot be smelt.
It lies behind stars, and under hills,
And empty holes it fills.
It comes first, and follows after,
Ends life, ends laughter.

Without even thinking, Gollum
Answered, "Dark!" Then gave his.
Then, one after one, they
Challenged each other, each of
Gollum puzzles getting harder,
And he seemed to realize it.
He started stepping out of his boat
To get closer to Bilbo, "So, he
Can eat me," Bilbo cringed.
So, thank goodness, he thought
Of puzzle that was sure to stop
Gollum. In his frustration at not
Being able to beat Gollum, he
Had been slapping himself
All over tp alert himself.
Then he hit the ring in his pocket.
"What have I got in my pocket?"
He asked. "Not fair, not fair, that's
Not a real puzzle . . . so you must
Give me three chances." "Chance
Away," Bilbo grinned, feeling
More confident. "Hands?" "Wrong!"
"Knife?" "Wrong! This will be your last chance."
Then Gollum shouted out a series
Of random words, all the while
Growing ever more angry.
That cause Bilbo to back up
Against the wall and point his
Knife at Gollum. Gollum must
Have taken the knife as an
Indication of his defeat.

He gave in, and didn't argue when
Bilbo demanded that Gollum
Fulfill his promise. "Now, you
Must show me the way Out of
This cave!" And Gollum did that,
All the while cursing and whining
That it was not not fair,
That his preciousness was missing.
Bilbo was almost beginning to
To feel sorry for this weird
Creature, but Gollum had
Led him to a large door, which
They both struggled to pry open.
The door gave, and Bilbo slid
Through, as Gollum stayed
Behind, still whining, and in the
Brighter light, Bilbo could see
Goblins milling about. One of
Them grumbled, "Look what's
Poppy out. Grab it" Bilbo
Manged to avoid the goblin,
And to quickly slip on his ring.
In prying his way through the
Tight door, he had lost most
Of his shirt brass buttons
Which no longer seeing Bilbo,
Started the goblin picking up the
Buttons. But Bilbo was oblivious
To this comic scene, he had Escaped!

Bilbo was almost giddy as he
Raced away from all the confused
Goblins. The giddiness faded
As his running legs weakened
And his hunger grew. He was
Finally forced to nap, with his
empty stomach, until late
The next day. What he saw, when

He joined his friends might
Have been funny had it not been
So scary. There were the dwarfs
Straddling the lower branches
Of several pine tree. And there
Was Gandalf hiding behind the
Huge trunk of that tree, waiting
Until the others had gain height
Before he started to ascend.
Bilbo moved up beside him
And asked, "What's the danger?
Why is everyone climbing this
Tree?" Gandalf started, and
Looked around to see where
Bilbo's voice had come from.
Bilbo, realizing that he had
His ring on, moved off behind
Another tree trunk, removed
The ring, and called out,
"It's me, Bilbo, I escaped the
Goblins." It took Gandalf a
Moment to register what he was Seeing,
Then he rushed over, Picked up
Bilbo and hugged him. "It's
Bilbo, he's alive!" The dwarfs
Shouted their happiness, and
And urged him and Gandalf
To hurriedly climb the tree.
Gandalf, because of his height,
Had no trouble grabbing
A lower branch, then reached
Back and pulled Bilbo up
After him. Then he shoved him
Towards a higher branch.
"Wargs, or what bad wolves
Are called. Can you hear them?"
Bilbo listened, and what he
Heard, made him shudder,

And tried to climb higher up
The tree. "We only have dogs,
Small dogs, in Hobbit Land."
As the Wargs came into view,
Gandalf encouraged his men,
"There are many of the,
And they'd love to feast on us,
But Wargs can't climb trees.
Trolin, make sure your people
Are as high as they can get.
And, all of you, cover your eyes.
Then he struck his wan against
The trunk of the tree, and
Sparks showered down on the
Growling Wargs. It didn't take
Long for the burning, yapping
Wargs To scatter back into the Woods.
But suddenly some goblins came rushing up,
And actually started laughing.
Now Bilbo was getting smoke in
His eyes, And they were
Burning, and the goblins
Continued laughing, and that
To one of their terrible songs.
"Oh no!" shouted Gandalf,
It's Goblins, and goblins aren't
Afraid of fire. They use fire
To torture their food. Hurry,
Climb higher! And he hurried
Himself ss the arriving goblins began singing.

Fifteen birds in five fir-trees,
Their feathers are fanned
In a fiery breeze!
But funny little birds,
They have no wings!
O what shall we do
With the funny little thing?

Roast 'em alive, or stew them in a pot;
fry them, boil them, and eat them hot?

Then they stopped singing,
And Gandalf shouted out,
"Run little boys if you can.
Then, get away, little boys!
For naughty little boys
Who play with fire get
Punished." But the goblins Ignored him
And began singing again.

Burn, burn tree and fern!
Shrivil and scorch! A fizzing torch
To light the night for our delight.,
Ya hey!
Bake and toast 'em, fry and roast 'e
till beards blaze, and eyes glaze!
Til hair smells, and skin cracks,
fat melts, and bones black
in cinders lie
beneath the sky!
So dwarves shall die!
And light the night for our delight,
Ya hey!
Ya harri-hey!
Ya hoy!

And with that Ya hoy, many of
The trees caught fire, and soon
The blazes were beginning
To reach Bilbo and the dwarfs.
But Gandalf had climbed
To the top of his tree
And lightening flashed from
His wand and fire lit up
The goblins all their weapons,
Sending them, yelling and Screaming away

From the Burning trees. Just at that
Moment, a giant eagles swept down and snatch up
Gandalf, and Instantly afterwards, other eagles
Snatched up the dwarfs. And the Terrified d
Bilbo was the last
To be rescued. "Not by my neck!,
He screamed. His rescuing
Eagle laughed, "I could have
Grabbed the Other end."
Bilbo started to Object to that
But he looked back and saw all
Those trees burning, and
He apologized instead,
"Sorry sir eagle, Bilbo Baggins,
At your service!"

It wasn't long after Bilbo's
Eagle deposited him on a
Stone perch on the top of
A high hill that another eagle
Arrived, announcing, "The Lord
Of the Eagle bit you bring
Your prisoners to the Great
Shelf." More eagles flew in
And grabbed Bilbo and the
Dwarfs and carried them into
The air again. This time Bilbo's
Eagle was kinder. He clutched him
By the back of his coat. And,
In no discomfort this time, he
Began almost enjoying the
Ride. He looked out over
At the distant mountains
And over the valleys below.
He had certainly never seen
Such magnificent view in
His Hobbit Land. Maybe
Adventures weren't so awful

After all. After Bilbo was set
Down on the Great Shelf,
He noticed Gandalf and the
Lord of the Eagles were in
Serious discussion. They seemed
To know each other very well.
This is what Bilbo overheard.
"Yes, Gandalf, we can continue yo
On your journey to where you
Want to go, but we will never
Fly you anywhere near men
With their terrible bows." Gandalf
Understood and agreed. But
Now Bilbo was no longer Interested.
I whatever adventure Lay ahead.
He had just spied
The dwarfs were eagerly gobbling
Wild food that the eagles
Had brought from the valley below.
So, Bilbo became
One of the eager gobblers.
And thus ended his adventures
On Misty Mountain. He Settled
Down to a much needed and\ Dream-filled Sleep, dreams
Of his home in Hobbit Land,
And to his surprise,
He found himself mumbling in
His sleep, "I wonder why I
Can't remember what my home
Looks like, and I can't smell my tea."

ACT III

SCENE VII: QUEER LODGINGS

They all bid the Lord of the
Eagles farewell, and walked
Carefully down a steep trail,
Until they came to gentler land
Where they found a small,
And safe cave, where Gandalf
Explained what was going
To happen next. "You recall, I
I promised to bring you are safely
Over these first mountains, and
I have done so, but now
I have other business to attend to, So
I must soon bid you farewell.
The dwarfs groaned and looked
Most distressed, and Bilbo looked
Even more concerned. Before
I leave you, there is someone
I know who might help you.
He won't come to us, so we
Must go to him. He is the one
Who made the steps On the great Rock,
Carrock I believe it is called, and that is where we
Will met him. And that was plan,
And all the treasures the dwarfs
Offered him, could not change his
Mind. On the way to Carrock,
Gandalf cautioned all.
"The person who lives at Carrock
Is a great person, so we must treat
Him as such. You must be very
Polite when I introduce you,
And you must approach him
Two by two, and you must never

Anger him or Heaven knows what
Will happen!" "And what more
Must we know about him," asked
Bilbo," trembling. As he asked.
"His name is Beorn, and he is
A skin-changer." "You mean he
Changes his skin to hair,"
Asked Bonfur. "Not unless his
Hair is bear hair, and sometimes
He is a giant man, and strong
As an ox. No one know where
He came from, but now he lives
In Oakwood, in a great wooden
House, and he keeps cows and
Horses that almost as amazing
As he is. the talk to him and
They work for him and help him
Care for his great fierce bees."
"Bees," asked Bilbo, and do they
Make Honey?" "The best, almost
Taste like ale." At that all the
Dwarfs perked up. "And he has
Lots of hives?" asked Bombue.
"You'll see when we get there,"
Concluded Gandalf, then added,
"I once saw him sitting on
Carrock, staring at the moon,
Growling in the tongue of bears,
"The day Will come when they
Will perish, and I will go back."
That was when I knew he had
Once come from the mountain
Himself." On the way to Carrock,
They passed through a field
Of flowers where large bees
Were sucking honey from
The blossoms, "I can taste it
Now!" shouted Gloin. Smacking

His lips. Bilbo's lips were Smacking too,
"I never tasted honey that was not only
Sweet, but also like ale. Hurry
Up fellows! Let's get some ale.

Eventually, they came to high
Hedge that the dwarfs could
Not see over. "You fellows wait
Here, while Bilbo and I look
For another way to get in."
"Why Bilbo? I'm taller. Why not
Me?" objected Ori. Gandalf
Laughed, "Because Bilbo's the
Burglar, and he can steal some
Honey." Ori seemed hesitant,
And before he could respond
Further, Gandalf Hurried Bilbo
Along with him, until the came
To a half open Gate.
As they Slipped through,
Bilbo repeated Ori's Question.
"Why me, Gandalf?" "Because you are
More inquisitive. You Ask
More questions, and maybe
We'll learn something when
Beorn answers. Bilbo
Nodded and smiled. Then
He asked himself, "Maybe
I should ask if I should even
Be on this wild journey."
Gandalf smiled also, and
Looked at Bilbo knowingly.
But all such questions ceased
When they entered Beorn's yard.
There were the cows and the
Horses attending the giant bee Hives.
"Ugh! They don't look
Dangerous, so you can be off,"

A large man said to the cows and
Horses. Then he laughed,
Put down his ax an lumbered
Forward. Gandalf obviously wasn't
Intimidated, "I am Gandalf, the \
Wizard." "Never Heard of you.
And who is this Little fellow?"
Gandalf started to speak, but
Bilbo got up his Courage and answered first.
"I am Bilbo Baggins, at your
Service." Gandalf smiled at
Bilbo, and turned back toward Beorn.
"Perhaps you've heard
Of my good cousin, Radagast,
Who lives near the southern border of
Mirkwood.?" "Not a bad fellow as wizards go.
What do you want from me?"
"We have lost our luggage, and
Nearly lost our way, and in need
Of whatever help or advise
You can can give us. We had
A rather bad Time with goblins."
"Goblins!" barked Beorn, and
Why did you go near them?"
"It's a long story," sighed Gandalf.
"So, Maybe you'd better come Inside and tell me."
They followed the giant bear-like man through
A dark door and into a large hall
With a large fireplace burning
In the middle. As they sat down,
Gandalf began his story, "I was
Coming through the forest with
A friend or two . . ." "A friend or Two?
How many?" "Well, to tell The truth,
I didn't want to bother You." "Bother me,"
Beorn Encouraged, so, names.
But Beorn stopped him. "Call them!" T
Gandalf began Listing all the dwarfs by he Gandalf

Whistled, and eventually the Dwarfs started filing in,
Two by two, until Trolin followed last,
And bowed and spoke up loudly, "Thorin, of
Oakenshield, at your Service."
"I don't need your Service, but but if you are
No friends of goblins, and you'll do mischief in my land,
Then after your tale is finished.
Perhaps we can have some dinner . . .
"At that, the dwarfs Jumped up and started shouting.
"Yes, dinner, dinner! We're Starving."
"And will there be Honey?" begged Bilbo.
At that, The giant bear, Beorn laughed
Heartily and bade his clever dogs
To bring what seemed like
Mountains of food to be spread
Upon the, there were may stuffed
Dwarfs and and one very sleepy
Hobbit, laying their heads upon
The table. Then, Bilbo woke

With a start. The Dwarfs
Were siting around the fire,
And presently, they began to sing.

The wind was on the withered hearth,
But in the forest stirred no leaf:
There shadows lay by night and day
And dark things silent crept beneath.

The wind came down
From mountains cold,
And like a tide it roared and rolled;
The branches groaned,
The forest moaned,
And leaves were laid upon the mold.

The wind went on from West to East;
All movement in the forest ceased.

But shrill and harsh across the marsh
In whistling voices were released.

The grasses hissed, there tassels bent,
The reeds were rattling—on it went
O'er shaken pool under heavens cool
Where racing clouds were torn and rent.

It passed the lonely Mountains bare
And swept above the dragon's lair:
There black and dark
Lay boulders stark
And flying smoke was in the air.

It left the world and took its flight
Over the wide sea of the night.
The moon set sail upon the gale
And stars were framed in leaping light.

Bilbo began to nod again. Suddenly,
Upstood Gandalf. "It's time for
Us to sleep, but not I think for
Beorn. In this hall we can rest
Sound and safe, but I warn you
As Beorn has said, you must not
Stray outside when the sun has set.
It was full morning when Bilbo
Awoke, and he found that
Dori was yelling at him,
"Get up, Lazy bones, it's time to
Eat breakfast!" "Breakfast?
Where is breakfast?" "Outside,
But mostly inside of us, but
What is left is on a table there."
Bilbo hurried outside and gobbled
Up a few scrapes of food. "And
Where is Gandalf?" "Oh, out there,
Somewhere," answered Gloin."

But they saw no signs of Gandalf
Until just before sunset. He walked
Into the hall, where Bilbo and
The dwarfs were having supper,
Being waited on by Beorn's
Wonderful animals. Of Beorn,
Then had heard nothing since
The night before, and they were
Getting puzzled. "Let me eat first,"
Complained Gandalf. "I haven't
Had a bite since breakfast."
Having eaten his fill, he started
Answering their questions. "I
Have following bear-tracks,
And they seem to be heading
Back where we came from being
Bothered by all those Wargs and
And Goblins." "What shouted
Trolin, that means he's bringing
Our enemies down on us! I thought
You said he was not a friend of
Theirs." "Don't be silly," countered
Gandalf. "Go to sleep, your fear
Is affecting your think." Gandalf
Was right, the next morning,
Beorn woke them. "What, you're
Still here? He picked up Bilbo,
And laughed, poking his belly,
"Getting fat on my good food,
Yes the goblins would really
Like you now." Bilbo gasped,
But laughed along with Beorn
After he was let down. Gandalf
Followed up on the laughter
By smiling at Bilbo. "Yes, our
Great Burglar would never get
Caught anyway." Thorin was
Obviously getting impatient.

"But what did you find last
Night?" Beorn sighed, "Yes,
I know you need to know. I
Caught a terrified goblin who
Was almost angry enough to
Complain that some monster
Wizard had chopped off his
Great Goblin. He wasn't angry
Very long." Beorn finished
His story with a smile. Bilbo
Was caught between satisfaction
And concern about the great
Bear's comfort at dispatching
The goblin. "Then what did you
Do with the goblin," asked Bilbo.
"Come outside and see," was
Beorn response. There, on a
Post was a goblin head. Then,
Satisfied with his show, Beorn
Described how he would carried
Out what he had promised to
Do for them. He would would
Provide them with ponies for
Each dwarf and Bilbo, and
A horse for Gandalf, and amble
food and the clothing they would
Need on the trail toward Mirkwood
You will find plenty
O water in streams along the,
But eat nothing you see along
The trail. And that is all the help
I can Give you brave travelers,
And especially the great burglar,
Bilbo Baggies. Bilbo opened his
Mouth to give thanks, but Thorin
Spoke first. "Great Beorn, you
Are more than generous. And
Should we come this way again,

We will surely bring you gold
From the dragon's lair." So
Off they went, out the gate
In front of Beorn's Great
Bee hive yard, and off to the
Right toward the trail through
Mirkwood and on upward
Toward the Lonely Mountain.
Beorn had warned them to
Be continually aware that the
Trail might sometimes be used
By goblins. That was why they
Were now riding in silence
But galloping rapidly where
The grass was smooth. As the
Trail wound upward, Bilbo
Notice fewer rabbits or deer,
And nothing looked edible
Alongside the trail. Thank
Goodness, they had plenty
Of food, so that didn't bother
Them. That afternoon, they
Had reached Mirkwood, and
Were resting "Now here is
Mirkwood, the greatest forest
Of the Western World. Look
About if you want, but then
We must prepare send these
Ponies back to Beorn as we
Promised. "Just the ponies,"
Objected Thorin, "What
About your horse?" "I am
Not sending it because I am
Riding it" By this, they knew
That Gandalf was leaving them
Again, and they were in despair.
But nothing they said changed
His mind. As he had said before,

I have other business to attend to,
But I am leaving Bilbo Baggins,
The great burglar with, and as I
Have said, he will be of great
Help to you." With that, he gave
One of his enigmatic smiles,
And said no more. But Thorin
Wasn't smiling when he tried
Again to get Gandalf to stay
With the troop, and Bilbo didn't
Feel that he had been all that
Useful either. The next morning,
Gandalf bid his farewells, and
Was gone. The troop spent some
Time distributing the supplies
Among the ponies. Bilbo called
After the retreating Gandalf,
"But I want to go with you."
And Gandalf responded, "But
I need you to look after the
Dwarfs for me." "But I can
Barely look after myself," Bilbo
Protested, and Thorin nodded

SCENE VII: FILES AND SPIDERS

They walked in single file
Leading to a gloomy tunnel
Of trees outside of which
They could see flickering lights.
"What kind of insects would
Have multiple eye like those
Insects seem to have? Asked
Birfur. "Spiders would," suggested
Ori. Bilbo jumped in, "Well,
They're tiny spider if they're

Spiders." "So now our mighty
Burglar is an expert on spiders?"
"Maybe an expert on keeping
Dwarfs from scaring themselves
Before they go to sleep later
Tonight. That quietened the
Fearful speculation until they
Settled for the evening meal,
Which was hearty, since their
Food supplies were yet amble.
But Thorin, ever the careful
Leader, "Don't over-eat. We
Still have a long way to go!"
That didn't stop the piggish
Dwarfs, though Bilbo did
Compliment Thorin, "Listen
To him, fellows, He's just being
Responsible." Thorin looked
At Bilbo, puzzled look on his
Face. Several nights later,
Bilbo cried out, "There's a boat
Against the far bank! Now why
Couldn't have been on our
Side? We could use it to carry
Ours supplies now that we have
No ponies" Various dwarfs
Suggested various way of obtaining
The needed boat. They tried
Looping a rope over the boat's
Front end, but it slipped off
Many times. Finally, Bilbo looped
The rope over a tree stump beyond
The boat, and then taking a deep
Breath, was able to jump into
The icy water, and hand over hand,
Pull himself into the boat.
He received a cheer for this clever
Effort, and even a smile from

Trolin. Then, placing their supplies
Into the boat, they pulled it
Along behind them in the creek.
Later, toward evening, Nori called
Out, "There's a deer across the
Creek!' Quickly, the dwarfs shot
Arrows after arrow at the fleeing deer.
And most of their arrows were
Lost before they heard Thorin's
Command to stop." "You fellows
Should learn to listen to your leader,"
Bilbo cautioned. That earned some
Sorry looks from some of the dwarfs,
And one jeer at Bilbo by Gloin.
Thorin smiled, but then quickly
Covered his smile. The food became
Less and less each day along
The dreary trail, until the mood
Elevated when the trail ahead
Turned downward, leading them
Between massive oaks. At least it was
Less gloomy. But Thorin wasn't
Happy. "Is there no end to this
Accursed forest! Someone needs
To climb one of these trees,
And tell us when this forest
Will end!" He looked at Bilbo,
That someone meant the great
Burglar, Bilbo. "Bilbo Baggins,
At your service," he mocked,
And scooted up the nearest
Tree trunk until he came to
The top of the tree. Looking
Around, he shouted back down,
"The forest goes on forever
In all directions. His discouraging
Report made the others as
Discouraged as he was. So, on

They trudged growing more
Hungry as they went. Until
Bombue called out, "I Thought
I saw a twinkle of light in the
Forest off to the side, and then
Another, and then another. But
Then the lights flickered out,
And Bombue cried out," Maybe
There's food at that light light.
So, they all started crawling to
See many people eating and
Laughing about a fire, and they
They couldn't help dashing over
to partake of the feast. Bilbo was
At the pack, and looking ahead,
He told himself, "This doesn't
Look right." So, he pulled out
His ring and slid it onto his finger.
Then he called out to his friends,
"Dwalin, Kili, Dori, Nori, Ori,
Oin, Gloin, Bifur, Bofur, Bombue,"
But no one answered, he was all
Alone. "I can't do anything in this
Dark, so I had better just wait
Until I can see." And that's what
He did, but briefly, for suddenly,
He felt his legs being bound up
With sticky threads, and then
He could see that is was a giant
Spider that was binding him.
All he could see was its eyes, so
He slid out his dagger and
And the dagger's blue light
Came so now he could see, so
He stabbed the giant spider
In one of its eyes. The spider
Tumbled backwards, and Bilbo
Was able to disentangle his

Legs from the spider web.
"I'm free, you wicked web
Monster. Guess You never
Faced the a Mighty Sword-Master
Hobbit!" Then he laughed,
And looked admiringly at his
Small dagger. You really stung
The old spider, now I'm going
To name you *Sting*. So, *Sting*,
Let's get to work! But maybe
I'd better slip on my ring. What
Can't see me, can't eat me,
Before I sting it. So now to
Find my friends. With is sword
Light, he could see the giant
Spider web stretched across
The many limbs of a massive
Tree, and there all about it
Were dozens of giant spiders
Busy entangling his friends.
He didn't waste time counting,
But he guessed they were
All there bundle tightly in
Their spider web cocoons.
They couldn't see him, so
He had no trouble stabbing
Them one by one. At first,
They froze, not knowing what
Was happening. Then they
Panicked, and fled away.
Bilbo then took off his ring
And began cutting away his
Friend's cocoons, that dropped
To forest floor. It was a long
Drop, but the soft cocoons
Must have protected the dwarfs.
He was sure of it when he heard
An "Umph!" as each hit the ground.

"Bilbo! Bilbo, how did you do this?
And where are all the spiders?"
Then, as he cut them from their
Cocoons, he urged them to hurry
Back to the trail. "I scared them away,
But many more will be coming
Back, and we need to form a
Fighting-circle to protect ourselves.
Then Trolin took charge. "Great
Work, Bilbo. Let's do what the
Hobbit says!" So, soon the
Were in their tightly bound circle,
Swords out and ready. "Great!"
Said Bilbo. But I'm going to
Circle around them, and they'll
Be so busy with you, they won't
What's killing them from behind.
"And they won't see me either,"
He told himself as he put on
His ring. "Now for some real
Adventuring!" Then sneaking up
Behind them, he began stinging
Them in rapid succession, and
Soon those that he and the dwarfs
Hadn't killed, dashed away. And
Then Bilbo followed them far
Enough so the dwarfs couldn't
See him slip off his ring. But they
Did see him when he came back
To the circle, hugged him, and
Pounded him on his back, shouting
"Bilbo, Bilbo the Great Spider-
Killer!" "And you, my friends,
are going to be know as The Great
Bilbo killers," he laughed.
And Thorin was also laughing, but then
Turned Serious, "We will rest
Briefly, and mv on up the trail

149

Until we can be certain the spider
Won't start chasing us again."
"No need To worry, Captain,
Not with the Spider-killer
With us," said Dori. So, two days
Later, rest they did,
Until sufficiently rested, they
Hoped to come to the end of the
Mirkwood Forest and continue
On to their Treasure cave.
But that wasn't to be. Their
Rest was interrupted by
Large Wood-elves, who bound
Them and dragged away toward
There Great Cave some miles
Withing Mirkwood. Bilbo hadn't
Rested well. "Am I just exhausted
From my adventure or bragging
On myself from being the
Spider-Killer. It was a good thing
He was awake. When one of the
Wood-elves flung a boot at him,
He doubled up in a ball and
Rolled over the edge of the trail
Deep into a ditch. "Never mind,"
Another Wood-elf ordered,
You can come back later
And pick him up." After the
Were gone, Bilbo slipped on his
Ring and followed the Wood-elves
With their dwarf prisoners. The
Wood-elf cave was large, with
Many small room off to the
Sides. In the middle of the cave
Sat the King of the Wood-elves,
"How come you come to steal
Our gold and jewels? And where
Are your treasures? Thorin was

Growing angry, but he remained
Calm. "We have no gold and
Jewels. In fact, we are so poor,
We are starving, so we come
To beg" But the Wood-elf King
Obviously wasn't satisfied,
So Thorin shut and would say
No more. That made the King
Even angrier, so he ordered
His men to lock each of them
In separate cells, and lock
Thorin in a cell even further
Down in the darkest dungeon.
"And feed them daily, bread
And water, and tell them they
Can only come out of their
Cells when they tell me
What I want to know."

SCENE IX: BATTLES OUT OF BOND

A Woods- elf did back looking for
Bilbo, but he did not find him.
He had already slipped on his ring,
So he couldn't find him. The
Wood-elf laughed, "I hope a
Goblin ate him. Serves him right
For not doing what he was told."
Bilbo followed the Wood-elf
Through the woods and into
The large hall of the Wood-elf
King. He was angry and sneering
Down at Thorin and the other
Dwarfs. "Why have you come
Attacking my friendly people?
I suspect, being a dwarf, you

Are trying to trick my innocent
Elves and steal what little we
Have. Bilbo noticed that Trolin
Was holding in his anger, and
He knew why. These Wood-elves
Well off, cruel in their ways
Of attacking and robbing weaker
People. Bilbo also noticed
Maybe a dozen empty wine
Bottle along side the Wood-elf's
Richly adorned thrown. "No,
Great Wood-elf King. We did
No come to rob, we came to beg.
We were attacked by goblins, by

Off to the slaughter!
We dwarfs aren't crying,
And aren't afraid of dying,
Wargs, by spiders, and now

By your gallant warriors, who
Where only protecting their
Land." "Wow," Bilbo muttered
To himself. I haven't seen this
Side of the noble Leader of the
Dwarfs. He must be desperate
To fool the Wood-elf King."
But the Wood-elf King wasn't
Fooled. Even with all the empty
Wine bottle lying around his
Thrown, he still wasn't fooled.
He raged, "Who do you think
You are trying to fool me?
Claiming to lived and escaped
All those monsters, and only
Lost your lives, this is just another
Of you devious tricks. Here's
What's going to happen to you.

152

Guards, take these sneaky elves
And place each of them in
Separate cells with only bread
And water, and don't let them
Out till they tell me what I
Want to know!" he growled,
"And take Mister Trickster
Down to the last cell in
The deepest dungeon. I have
Special treatment in mind
For him. "Wow!" Bilbo whispered
Again. "I haven't seen this side
Of Thorin either. He isn't even
Frightened." Then Bilbo was
Even more impressed. At that
Moment Thorin commanded,
"Brothers, Sing brothers, sing!"
And they did!

Bread and water!
Bread and water!
Off to the slaughter!
So, give us bread and water!
We'll have lots of fun with our slaughter,
Bread and water!
Bread and water!
Bread and water!

With this brave mockery, the
King was enraged. "Bash them!
Bash them!" he demanded.
And the guards did, shouting as
They did, "Die! Die! Die!
To which Thorin Countered, "Live! Life! Live!"
And this went On until Iron cages were heard
Being slammed shut
Somewhere down a long ally.
Then, still with his key on, Bilbo

Tried to follow the brave singers,
But he he was being was blocked
By other guards at the door.

Frustrated, Bilbo checked out one
Of the side rooms. There, he
Found crates filled with empty
Wine bottlers and in straw bed,
And scraps of animal meat,
Cheese, greens, and fruit.
"At least Neither I nor my friends are going
Hungry," He said, happily,
While stuffing his Pockets and
Mouth with what he found there.
Then he Settled down for a good
Night's sleep. early next morning,
Bilbo found the guards had left
The keys to the dungeon on the
Doorway, so he slipped down the
Long corridor until he found two
Things. Two guards were playing
Dice, and from the empty bottles
And the way they wobbled, Bilbo
Knew they were half drunk.
So, he helped them along by
Knocking them on
The backs of their heads with his
Dagger handle. The dwarfs were
Happy to see him when he
Slipped his key off his finger,
And especially when he began
Stuffing food through the cell
Bars. "Bilbo, the Burglar bags our
Food! They shouted as they
Began eating their food. Then
Bilbo hurried further down to
Find Thorin, who was more

Eager to have Bilbo listen to
His instructions. "Make sure
You tell the others they must
Tell the Wild-elf King anything
About our going to recover our
Smaug-stollen teasures. After
That, Bilbo explored further along
The downward sloping corrridor.
He found a large trapdoor, which
When he opened it, down a
Twenty-foot drop was smoothly
Flowing water. "Ah ha!" he said to himself.
"This is where the food and empty wine
Bottles get sent down to the river,
But to where,?" he wondered.
"Never mind, my friends and I
Have plenty to eat, and these
Halfway tipsy elves won't know
That we're not half-starving and
And looking for a way to escape."
"And more importantly, they
Don't even know that I exist!"

Now Bilbo wanted to know what
Wood-elfs had to offer whomever
They were selling to down-river.
As Bilbo followed them all day,
and all evening he saw that they,
In spite of their wine drinking,
They were hard and effective
Hunter, workers, and craftsmen
They stripped the animals, smoked
Their meat, cleaned and processed
Their hides into leather and fir.
Bilbo was impressed. He also
Whispered his thanks, "From all
Your hard work, you will be able
To buy all the wine you and your

Wood-elf King can drink, and
All the food my dwarf friends can eat."

Bilbo reported all this to Trolin,
"And who is buying all this stuff
Wherever?" "Let me explain.
Everybody all the way up to the
Dragon's cave knows about
All the treasure that is there. They
Also know that it belongs to us.
So, they will help us kill the
Dragon, and recover our treasure.
"Kill the dragon? You're going to
Do that!" "Us and you, your our
Hero now." Bilbo tried to laugh,
"So, I'm going sneak right up to
Smaug, secretly tickle him so
He sneezes away all his fire breath,
And he will just stand by weeping
While we carry away all our
Treasure?" "There you go said
Thorin, "I knew you would figure
A way." Bilbo sighed, and
Changed the subject. "And all
The other eager Treasurer Luster-
Afters will just wait for us to give
Them their share?" No," said Thorin,
Becoming serious again, "They will
Try tp take it from us us."
So, that was the story, and that was
The challenge for Bilbo, so now all
He could do was wait for
The next exchange of goods
From the Wood-elvs to Forest Lake
Town to See how it was done.
Or should he take a chance he would
Get right and do it right away?
The cramped and cold

Dwarfs said do it now!
So, Bilbo watched as many elves
Shoved wooden crates loaded with
Empty wine bottles, smoked
Meat, skins and firs alongside
The dwarfs' Cells, and leave them
There. Bilbo guessed they would be shoved
Ddown the trapdoor
Into the slowly moving stream by the
Two riders of the crates to
River Town. "So far so good," thought
Bilbo. And it was.In the dark of early more,
The same two guards whom Bilbo had conked on the
backs of their heads came to dump the
Crates down the trapdoor. As before,
Bilbo added to their tipsiness by taps
On the backs of their heads.
Then Bilbo used their cell keys
To free the Dwarfs and assist them
In removing enough goods
For the dwarfs to fit inside.
As Bilbo hoped, the guards were
Still too tipsy to notice
That the dwarfs cells were empty.
"Oh you sneaky burglar," laughed Tholin,
"You've done it again" "You mean, you
Lucky burglar," Suggested Bilbo.
Whether their Balancing job was accurate, or it
Was Bilbo's luck again, the guards
Seemed satisfied that crates were
All equally balanced, so, the guards
Shoved the dwarf loaded crates
Through the trapdoor, and Bilbo
Was relieved that the guards
Seemed not to notice the many
"Umphs" when the crates hit the
Water. Then Bilbo Jumped
Through right after, and landed

On top of the last crate. Since the
Guards were on the first
To two crates, Bilbo missed them,
And he was careful not to reveal
His invisible self by a suspicious
"Umphs." Then it was smooth riding
All the way to Lake Town
As Invisible Bilbo rode quietly
Halfway back down the row of
Crates from the two guards.
On the left he noticed the thick
Forests of trees began to thin,
To become grape orchards and
Grain fiends. By early evening,
The two guards had jumped up
Onto the bank and were, with
Great effort hauling, the crates
Up on the shallow shore.
Then, they took off Over a
Great Bridge, and onward toward
The center of Lake Town,
Where Bilbo assumed they
Would do more heavy drinking.
Only then did Bilbo start helping
The dwarfs out of their cramped
Confinement. They all groaned
And complained, but Thorin
Quieted them. "Just think, you
Whining wimps, our hero, Bilbo
Wasn't warmly concealed inside
The crates, he was not doubt
Freezing being exposed on top
Of these crate. The dwarfs
Grudgingly thanked Bilbo, and
Bilbo didn't bother to tell them
How happy he had been, lying
Half asleep, staring at the stars
That were brighter than any he

Ever seen over his Hobbit Home.
"A hero has to be tough," he
Stated, trying not to laugh.
Then they trudged over the
Bridge, and up to what must be
The gate-guards' housing.
Thorin marched up, as erect as
He was able, to guard lounging
by the housing door, announcing loudly,
"I am Thorin, son of Thrain, son of Thror King
Under the Mountain!" The guard first snapped to
Attention, and then apparently Seeing
Thorin's be-strageled Condition, hesitated a
Moment, and the called inside.
"Chief, you'd better come out here!'
As the guard chief was Showing up,
Thorin barked even Louder,
"I am Thorin, New King Under the Mountain,
Take me to Your City Master!
The Chief Guard hesitated a moment, and
Then demanded, "Surrender your Weapons!"
"We have no weapons.They were stolen from us
By the Wood-elfs, Anyway, we Come in peace.
Please Take us to Your City Master."
The Chief Guard hesitated no longer.
He said respectfully, "He at
Feast, but I will take you to him."
When Bilbo, in the rear, all the
Dwarfs were led into a large inn,
The large man at the center table
Jumped to his feet, and did a small
Bow. "It is my honor, New King
Under the Mountain. Please, please,
Have your men sit at my table!
Thorin stated to ask his men to
Sit themselves around the table,
But, obviously, their huger was
"We have just escaped from the

Wood-elf King, And he didn't feed
Us very well." The City Master
Nodded, sympathetically.
"I can imagine!" he nodded at the
Two Woode-elfs seated across the
Room. "And they don't smell
Too well either. But sit, sit eat!"
The dwarfs were already doing
That vigorously. Thorin thanked
The City Master, but before he
Started eating, said softly, "Let
Me introduce Bilbo Baggins of
Hobbit Town. It was he who
Rescued us, singledhandedly
From that dreadful monster
Wood-elf King!" "Hardly by
Myself," Bilbo blushed. "Yes,
By himself, but always modest."
Bilbo managed to appear modest,
While he was bursting with pride.
But he did managed to hold in
His pride, and while eating he
Was able to ask Thorin why
The City Master was being so nice
To them. Thorin whispered,
Between bites, "The City men
Also want their cut of the dwarfs'
Treasures, so I'm afraid all is
Not going to go so easily after
We recover our treasure."
"Oh No," muttered Bilbo. "The
Great Hero just want's to go home!"

The Town Master became
Even more gracious, "Here's
What I'm going to do brave
And so cruelly victimized
Travelers. For your continued

160

Journey up to your home on
The mountain, I'll have waiting
For you, ample ponies for your
People and the food I am
Giving you." For this. Thorin
Could only bow deeply. And
So, re-outfitted, and for the
Dwarfs and Bilbo, well fed,
They headed happily up the
Mountain. But, as Bilbo looked
Up the steep trail toward the
High Mountain, he shamefully
Whispered to himself,
"You fellows might yet be happy.
You are going home. But, it's been
So long, I'm not sure I had
A home, but I am sure
That what's up in at mountain,
Won't make me feel at home."

SCENE XI: ON THE DOORSTEP

It took three days, after crossing
The river, unloading on t he bank,
And ridding on their ponies over
Animal-empty fields that they
Finally started going on an ever
Steepening It was here that Bilbo
Let his worry turn into complains.
"My fanny hurts from riding
This bouncing pony! I'm going
To walk." Then the dwarf who
Had been carrying Bilbo on his
Shoulders, complained, "How
Do you think I felt when I was
Being your pony?" Bilbo laughed,

161

And the climb continued on,
Until the steepness of the trail
Made any casual conversation
Difficult. Blank blank did say
That he remembered Thorin
Saying that there would be
Trees and green grass along
The way. "Probably Smaug
Breath seared it," suggested
Gloim. Thorin hushed that
Pessimistic comment, and
Silence seemed a better behavior
From them on. But then soon,
"Too soon," muttered Bilbo,
They came to the *Desolation
Of the Dragon,* And they were
Come at the waning of the Year.

It took three days, after crossing
The river, unloading on the bank,
And ridding on their ponies over
Animal-empty fields that they
Finally started going on an ever
Steepening It was here that Bilbo
Let his worry turn into complains.
"My fanny hurts from riding
This bouncing pony! I'm going
To walk." Then the dwarf who
Had been carrying Bilbo on his
Shoulders, complained, "How
Do you think I felt when I was
Being your pony?" Bilbo laughed,
And the climb continued on,
Until the steepness of the trail
Made any casual conversation
Difficult. Blank blank did say
That he remembered Thorin
Saying that there would be

Trees and green grass along
Smaug-Breath seared it,"
Suggested Gloin. Thorin hushed
That pessimistic comment, and
Silence seemed a better behavior
From them on. And then soon,
"Too soon," muttered Bilbo, they
Came to the *Desolation of the Dragon,*
And they would Come
At the waning of the Year.

But the dwarfs were anything
But pessimistic, the were
Optimistic, and when dwarfs
Are optimistic, they have to sing.
Bifur started it off, and then
All the other joined in.

Smaug, Smaug, Smaug
You burnt out bit of old rag,
We don't like to brag,
But we've got your butt in our bag!

So, Smaug, Smaug, Smaug,
We're charging your cave
Waving our victory flag.
That tells all the world,
Once it's unfurled,
That all your belching-fire jaws now sag,
You worn out, worn out old Smaug.

They reached the skirts of the
Mountain without meeting any
Danger, so they just to be certain
There was no unseen danger near,
Several dwarfs circled around
The other side of the mountain.
They found nothing, so the

Prepared to sleep in front of
A crack in the mountain side
"I smell smoke," warned Bilbo,
"And I think that means the
Dragon is breathing somewhere
Inside the the mountain."
Nevertheless, they went to
Sleep, and sleep soundly,
Being tired from their day's
Climb. Next day, Thorin
Sent several dwarfs circling
Higher and higher up the
Mountain trail, and they
Came back to lead the rest
To what they discovered.
Near the top of the mountain
Was what they hoped to find,
The Front Gate to Smaug's
Fire-breathing mouth, or at
Least the cave entrance to
To where somewhere inside
The hoped to find their
Treasure, and the successful end
To heir danger-filled journey.
"We're home! We're home!
They all shouted. And Bilbo
Could only hope "It will be a
Brief home away from home,
And not my final, my final home"

SCENE XII: INSIDE INFORMATION

But Thorin was intent in making
Their home cave, my cave,
So he argued, "Our Hero Burglar,
Please make our home your home

By taking a bag into our home cave
And gather whatever you'd like
For yourself, and bring it back here,
If you please, Mister Baggins."
Bilbo had to laugh, "At your service,
Mister Thorin," and hurried into the
The cave. But he quickly slowed down.
"That smells like dragon breath."
Then he remembered to put on
His ring. "Okay, smelly old Dragon,
Here I come to rob you of your
Treasures!" Then Bilbo was startled
By a great grumbling and a red glow
Up ahead, and from that red glow
A rumbling voice rose forth.
"Somehow, I can't see you, but
I can smell you, and you smell
Delicious, a bit dwarf-like. Well,
Show yourself, and partake of
My treasures." It took a moment
For Bilbo to gain the courage to
Speak up, at first in barely a
Whisper. But the he decided to
Play his burglar role. "No, no, I
Means yes, yes oh Great Master
Dragon, I happen to know some
Dwarfs, and although I have no
Interest in trinkets, they would
Probably be interested in maybe
A small gold cup." "Yes, yes,
Said Smaug. I believe I have
Such a thing. Come and get,
Mister Invisible but rich smelling
Mist Whatever. Bilbo saw that
The dragon was pointing at
A large chalice off to the side
Of himself. "Whispering to himself,
"I hope he won't be able to move

One of those big arms
Fast enough to catch me."
But before he moved forward,
The almost stumbled over
Something even more intriguing
Than he chalice. It about a foot long jewel
Partially covered by an old rag. Bilbo
Snatched it up and thrust int his pocket.
Then, feeling even more satisfied, he whispered.
"Here, here I come Mist Monster Dragon.
Smaug must have heard him for
Bilbo barely Had time to snatch up
The chalice, slip off this ring, and
Dash up and out Of the cave.
A wave heat and A roar of anger
Followed Bilbo As he burst out
Of the arms of the Cheering dwarfs.
But now the cheering faded.
Bifur asked Thorin, "Shouldn't
We go back into the cave. I don't hear
Smaug anymore. It must be
Warmer in there." "Yes," decided
Thorin, and take all your stuff
With you." Hastily, they did
That, and to their relief, not only
Was Smaug gone, the way to
The other side of the mountain
Seemed open. So, Throin asked
Bilbo to lead the way. It took a
While, but they were able to continue
On around the mountain.

SCENE XIII: FIRE AND WATER

Now Smaug had his own mission.
After leaving through the entrance

To his cave, as Thorin had suspected,
He circled around the mountain
And headed toward the men's town
Of Esgaroth. The men there were
Mostly merchandiser, not fighters,
So, when they saw Smaug approaching,
The did their best. But it was hardly
Enough. There shower of long
Arrows merely glanced off of the
Dragon's scaly hide and hurt him
No more than flies would have hurt
A rock. But Smaug's slashing tail
Swiped of the town's Great House
And scattered its occupants into
The distant river. And thus the
Town of Esgaroth was lost, and
Its people only hoped that aid
Would come from somewhere.

Smaug's next target was the
River-Town, the primary town
Of men, and their men were
Fighters. So, when the word
Went out that the dragon was
Approaching, those fighting-men
Drew their long arrows and sent
Them, arrow after arrow, against
The dragon's iron-scale hide,
Only to have them bounce off
Harmlessly. But then as their best
Bowman, Bard, was about to release
His arrow, the voice of an old thrush
Chirped in his ear, "Wait! Wait!
The moon is rising. Look for hollow
Of his left breast as he passes over
You, and strike there!" And without
Further thought, Bard released his
Arrow, and with a great hiss and

A last of fire, the was the end
Of Smaug, the last Dragon Under
The Mountain! But not of Bard.

Now Bart, the great Bowman,
Took charge, always in the name of
River-Town Master. "We know that
That is great treasure in the now
Dead dragon's cave, and it currently
In the hands of the dwarfs, who are
Are the descendants of the ancient
Miners who minded the goal,
That were made into all that jewelry
Waiting in that cave. Of course we
Will let those little dwarfs continue
Mining, but will take our share
Of those treasures and appreciate then
As we know best. But just in case
Those nuisance dwarfs don't cooperate,
Mister Town Master, send word
To the Wood-elfs to join us for
Their share." And all that was done.

Meanwhile, those nuisance dwarfs
Has thoughts and plans of their own.

SCENE XIV: THE GATHERING OF THE CLOUDS

But before they could begin them,
An old thrush few in, and began
Chirping that only, which no one could
Understand. But then the thrush changed
Into a large raven, and spoke in an ancient
That, nevertheless, all could understand.
"Know thou that Smaug is dead! And
Those who would have your treasure

Are gathering!" "Smaug is dead, Smaug
Is dead!" the dwarfs started shouting.
Now we are safe!" "Not so fast," warned
Thorin! "Didn't you hear what he said?
Enemies are gathering!" That silenced
The dwarfs, and perked up Bilbo's ears.
And he even like what he was telling
Himself. "Maybe this is a chance for
A clever burglar to do something to
Slow down this oncoming conflict."

The Next morning, a company of
Spearmen was seen marching up
The valley until they stood right
Before the Great Gate. As before,
Thorin hailed them in a loud voice.
"Who are you, and what do you want?"
This time, he was answered. "Hail,
Thorin, I am Bard, and I have
Come to parley." "And I am Thorin,
King of all Under The Mountain."
And he shot an arrow at Bard,
Which glanced off his shield,
To which Bard responded with,
"Consider yourself besieged!" After
Which, he and the Wood-elf King
Marched away.

SCENE IV: A THIEF IN THE NIGHT

Now the days passed slowly,
And the dwarfs spent their time
Gathering recording the treasure,
And Bilbo spend gathering memories
When his tummy didn't so need
Filling. But Thorin was more concerned

With memories of the Arkenstone of
Thrhin, and constantly reminding
The dwarfs to look for it. On continually
Hearing this, Bilbo wonder again
Why this jewel, though obviously
Beautiful, that he use, wrapped in
Old cloth, was so important to Thorin.
Somewhat relieved, the dwarfs
Reminded Thorin the great
Numbers of their fellow dwarfs
Would soon enough be arriving
From the South to aid them.
But Thorin, growing ever grim,
Only reminded them that
Bard and the Wood-elf King
Could get here sooner. With
That grim reminder, Bilbo
Decided it was time for him
To do what perhaps Gandalf
Would expect him to do.
"I wil now become the Burglar,
And steal Away in the night
And do heroic things." He approached
Bombur, "You look cold, friend
Bombur. Why don't you let
Me take your watch briefly, and
I'll call you out when I get too cold?
"Much appreciated, Mister Baggins,"
And back to the warm cave he went.'
And, feeling his pocket, to be sure
He had the Arkenstone of Thorin,
He headed down toward the camp
Of the dwarf's waiting enemies.
To get there, he had to cross
An icy stream, and he came out,
Shaking and shivering, one of
The camp guards wondered,
"Is that a fish flopping? I don't

Like fish." I am not a fish, Mister
Guard, I am Bilbo Baggins, come
To parley for the good of all.
Now, please take me to Mister
Bard." The guard must have
Been impressed by Bilbo's
Commanding voice, for he
Was immediately let to Bard

And the others. "Well, it that
Is the impressive Burglar the
Town Master told me about"
"And," said the Wood-elf King,
"I guess he's the one who stole
All my wine," To which Bilbo
Responded, "I only kept your
Wine away from you tipsey barge
Haulers. But enough social talk/
I have come to arrange a treaty
Among competing warrior,
Who should be cooperating
Rather than competing" "Well,
I'm impressed," said Bard,
"The thief comes diplomating.
Diplomate on, Mister Diplomat.
It was then that Bilbo pulled out'
The rag covered Arkenstone of
Thrhin, uncovered it, and flashed
It before all. "And now I give
To you the one peaceful weapon
That will bring the angry and
Powerful Thorin, King Under
The Mountain to his knees."
All gasped at the beauty of the
Jewel." And then, to Bilbo's
Startlement, a cloaked man
Was led through the crowd,
Being bowed to by all. But the

Old man stood tall, through off
The old cloak, and laughed,
"Well done, Mister Baggins, you
Have done just what I told Tholin
And the disbelieving dwarfs
What you would do." but
Bilbo was so relieved that
He ignored all the praise,
And, to the surprise of all,
Dashed over and hugged Gandalf,
The Great Wandering Wizard.
Pleased, and even more relieved,
Bilbo hurried back up the
Mountain trail to wake Bombor
And the eased off to the warm
Cave to seek his well deserved rest.

SCENE VI: THE CLOUDS BURST

Next morning, Thorin waited before
The Cave entrance. He challenged
Bard and the Wood—Elf King,
"I stand firm in what I have said,
So kindly be off." "But is there
Nothing I can show you to encourage
You to share your gold?" "Nothing!"
Replied Thorin, "Not even this!"
And then Bard drew out the
Shining Arkenstone of Thrain. Thorin
Gasped, "How did you get that?"
Then Bilbo braved easing up beside
The two. "I gave to them, I gave it
to avoid this terrible but unnecessarily
War" Thorin turned on Bilbo, grasped
Him and shook him, shouting "You
Miserable Hobbit! You miserable

Thief! I will through you off this
Mountain!" Then the commanding
Voice of Gandalf spoke up."
"Release the brave Hobbit,
And listen with an open mind
To what he has to tell you."
Bilbo began carefully to explain
His reasoning. "You remember you
Granted me my fourteen of the
Treasure. Well, I will return it all
To you if you will." Bilbo drew apart,
Hoping the Thorin would be more
Accepting of what Bard had to say,
But Thorin remained stubborn,
Even when Bard offered the the
Arkenstone. "Keep it! You get
No gold!" growled Thorin. "You are
Not making a very splendid King
Under the Mountain," said Gandalf,
But let's hope we will see otherwise
Soon." and he, the Wood-elf King,
and Gandalf headed back down the
Mountain. Bilbo followed, despondent,
Whispering, "Well, I did my best."

The next day, runners had come,
Stating the the dwarfs from Dale
Had come. Thorin welcomed them
Warmly and enthusiastically. With
Their size and heavy armor, they
Would certainly add to his strength.
They also informed him that
Bard and the wood-elves were
Preparing to head up the mountain.
And those same well prepared
Warriors suddenly came charging
Toward Thorin and his armed
Dwarfs. And Bilbo, off to the

Side, expressed his horror, "I
Have failed to be the peace maker
I so desperately wanted." But
Then there came hope. Gandalf
Bellowed, "Halt! Dread has come,
All of you, dwarfs and men alike,
A vast army of goblins and Wargs
Are in their train!" Then, suddenly,
Darkness began to fill the sky.
"Come," shouted Gandalf, "there
Is still time for council." This was
The plan they derived. Many units of
Dwarfs and men would join
Together to advance against
The oncoming foe, surrounding
Them and warring them down,
And this way, the enemy might
be defeated, and also, equally
Important, the dwarfs and men
Might become brothers. And
Thus the Battle of the Five
Armies began, and it was
Terrible and deadly, and many
Of the city and mountain warriors
Parishes. All day, the battle raged,
Until Bilbo heard a great voice
Calling, and he expressed his
Renewed hope, "This is the the
Thorin I knew and respected. This
Is my friend I hear calling." And
Call Thorin did," "To me, Elves and
Me! To me! O my kinfolk! Then the
Darkness was torn aside by the
Sunset., and Bilbo looked up
And cried," The Eagles! The
Eagles are coming! And Bilbo
And shouted his news so all
Could hear. But then he shouted

No more. A bolder came rolling
Down the mountain, smote him
Heavenly on his helm, and then
He knew no more, only painlessness.

SCENE THE VII: THE RETURN JOURNEY

When Bilbo returned to himself, he
Was literally by himself. When he
Could hear again, he heard dwarfs
Seemingly doing mundane chores.
Suddenly he was aware of a dwarf
Coming toward calling, "Where are
You, Bilbo.? Then Bilbo realized
That he still had on his ring. He
Slipped it, and said quietly, "I'm
Here." The dwarf almost stumbled
Over. "Come quickly! You are
Needed!" When they reached the
Gathering elves and Gandalf,
The Wizard looked relieved, but
Hurried Bilbo into a tent where
Thorin was waiting, weak and
With many wounds. "Hail, Thorin,
Hero of this great victory," Bilbo
Almost whispered. "Perhaps, said a
Thorin, also in a whisper. "But I
Did not call you to brag, but to
Apologize for how I spoke to you.
You have been the great burglar,
Not thief, so please forgive me'
And now I must bid farewell. And
With that, Thorin closed his eyes
And opened them no more. Bilbo
Sighed, closed his own eyes and
Turned away." They buried Thorin

The next day, deep within the
Mountain. And Bard laid the
Arkenstone on his chest. And
All in further sadness,
Bilbo and Gandalf bid farewell
To all the gathered dwarfs,
Dwalin, Kili, Dori, Nori, Ori,
Oin, Gloin, Bifur, Bofur, and
Bombue. And also to Dain,
Who had been crowned their
Chief. After moving down the
Trail, Bilbo stated, "I suppose
We will be going home?" But
They didn't get started until the
Next day. They had to load up
One fourteenth of the treasure.
Then the stopped on the beginning
Of the way home to talk to the
He would keep only two satchels
Gold coins. That would be more
Than he would ever need, and also
Too heavy to carry. And so they
Went on their uneventful way.

SCENE VII: THE LAST STAGE

Roads go ever ever on
Over rock and under tree
By caves where never sun has show,
By streams that never find the sea;
Over snow by winder sown,
And through the merry flowers of June,
Over grass and over stone,
And under mountains in the Moon.

Then Gandalf looked at Bilbo.

"What's the matter?" he asked
The matter was, there was
A crowd gathered at his very
Door, and his furniture and
Other goods were being carried
Out of his home. "Stop!" he
Shouted. "Those are my goods!
His gathered neighbors stared
At him, and some had to be
Convinced that he was alive.
As it turned out, Bilbo had
To buy back some of his own
Goods. "It's a good thing
I now have plenty of money."
Gandalf laughed. "After all,
You are the Grate Burglar."
Bilbo also laughed, "Great
Or not, I am certainly the
Happiest Hobbit in Hobbit
Land." and he went into
His neighbor empty home,
And intermediately made
Himself a cup of tea, and
Sipping it, he sang.

"Home, Home, Home,
There's not place like home.
The dragon is dead,
The goblins have fled,
And now I'm going to settle down
And put much flesh on my bone.
"Home, Home, Home,
There's not place like home.

And so it was for a while, then
Something surprising and pleasant
Happened. Bilbo's pleasant and
Accommodating nephew came

To stay with Bilbo. His name was,
Frodo, and his parents were
Bilbo's sister and husband.
They were school people,
And thus Frodo was inclined
Toward wanting to know about
The past and how that led
To the present, and now,
Particularly how the gentle,
Slightly overweight Bilbo came
Came to be called so many
Unbelievable names. But enough
Of Frodo's history, Bilbo
Welcomed him warmly "Oh my,
Who is this tall, handsome
Young Hobbit who has graced
My humble door?" Frodo looked
Around the large, richly decorated
Front room and decided to
Play humble. "Just a thirty-one
Year old never-done-much,
Never-been-anywhere Hobbit,
Who has come to stay with
His wonderful worldwide
Known uncle Bilbo, and kneel
In his presents." Saying this,
He made a low bow. Bilbo'
Couldn't contain himself, He
Burst out laughing, "Oh my,
Someone's been intertaining
You with tales of Bilbo, the
The Grate Diplomat. All
None sense, my boy, all
None sense." So, my uncle
Is not whom the traveling
Dwarf salesman call, Bilbe
The Grate Spider Killer,
Or Bilbo the Grate Goblin

Killer, or Bilbo the Grate
Eagle Flier?" Bilbo had
To pause at that one. Then,
In an almost whisper, "Was
That really me?' he wondered,
"Yes, I did feel Master
And above it all." Then he
Let his whisper fade away.
Then he made his voice
Firmer, "Don't look so
Worshipful, son. All that
Was just an old Hobbit's
Daydreaming. All none sense,
Non sense." Just then, Gandalf
Walked through the wide open
Door, and once again, Frodo
Was overcome with wonderment,
"Are you really Gandalf, the
Grate Wandering Wizard," he
Gasped. "No, just another old
Man come to gossip like old men
Do, with his old buddy Bilbo."
The shook hands, at that gave
Frodo time to recover. "And now
You've come to beg the Great
Bilbo to accompany you on
Anther great adventure. Gandalf
Only smiled at this, and then
Became serious, "No, old man
Gandalf has come to, not beg,
But request that Frodo, the soon
To be another grate adventurer
To to accompany him to and
Beyond places he has never
Even imagined existed" Hearing
That, Frodo started to laught,
But seeing the absolute serious
Expression on Gandalf's face,

He clamped shut his mouth.
The quickly, Bilbo roused himself,
And walked out and came back
Quickly, and handed an envelope
To Frodo, "Here, put this safely
In your deepest pocket. You will
Undoubtedly need it." "Yes, indeed,
Indicated Gandalf, and also choose
Anther Hobbit to adventure along
With you. You will need such a
Hobbit friend. "Yes indeed, echoed
Bilbo. "I certainly could have used
A Hobbit friend when I was
Terrified adventuring alone."
With all that said, Gandalf became
Less an old man, and more
A commanding leader, "Gather
Warm clothes, rain gear, have
Old uncle Bilbo supply us with
Some of that great food he
Hides away, and let us away!"
And off went Frodo, the new
Adventuring Hobbit, to gather
Up his Hobbit friend, to begin

THE TALE OF THE LORD OF THE RINGS.

And here stayed Bilbo the Hobbit,
Happy to sit back in his comfortable
Chair . . . until he decided to fix
Himself a hot cup of tea, "Ah, sweet tea!"

THE NARRATOR SUMMARIZES THE PLAY

Theater attendees, how might Shakespeare summarize this play? It's not a comedy, it's not a tragedy, and it's certainly not a history. It's a fantasy. And don't at least most fantasies have happy endings? But Bilbo was not just your typical fantasy hero, he was a reluctant, self-doubting hero, who nevertheless, behaved heroically. So, all you self-doubting theater going heroes, take a chance, and try to behave heroically.

Let there be dragons
Let there be trolls,
Let there be goblins,
All ull of holes,
When Bilbo the hero
Takes to the stage,
And, in an heroic rage,
Obliterate the monster's souls.

OTHER BOOKS BY THE AUTHOR

D. B. Clark is the author of: *The Way to Levi, 1ˢᵗEdition* (Kendall Hunt Publishing Co), *To Lead the Way, The End of Ohm, The Way Beyond, Self-Development and Transcendence, Ashes to Ashes, A Heaven of Hell, Thoughts Along the Way, The Way Beyond, Mother Rat & Love is Eternal, Left of the Right World, Beyond Forever, On the Shoulder of Giants* (all universe, Inc. *Forever Young, It could be Verse, Love and Roses, Mercury Smiled, Death: a Second Opinion, Poems from a Smorgasbord Mind, War: A Love-Hate, Relationship, Didactics, Affirmation, My Modern Haiku, Archives Volume One, The Way to L'vei, The Curse of Humorous Verse, These Poems be Philosophy, This Garden Earth, Chronicle One through Chronicle Thirty-Seven Honoring My Beloved Brother, Modern Metaphysical Verse, Paradise Reconsidered, My Best to You, Once Upon a Time, Wisdom in Verse, Sagacious or Silly Sayings, A Modern Mother Goose, More Medical Mirth, Even More Medical Mirth, Arguing With God, If I Learn, So Can You, A Poetic Fix for Politics, How it Really Happened, Terse Verse is Better Not Worse, Let Us War No More, These are My Best, Modern Aesop fables, Laughing at Myself, Poemmettes, Children Do Play with Dead Things, The New Devil's Dictionary, These are My Latest Best # Three, Four and Five, Once Upon a Time Again, Beyond Forever, Poemettes Three, Who an I, and Why?)*,The Autobiography of D. B. Clark, Sagacious or Silly Sayings # 2 Expanded, Once Upon a Time Three, *These are My Latest Best # Six, My Latest Best # Seven,* ((All by Lulu.com)*Poems will Make you Wiser, Aging, an Option, Dr Clark's Health Management Plan (These are My Latest Best # Six* all, lulu.com),The Autobiography of D. B. Clark, Sagacious or Silly Sayings # 2 Expanded, Once Upon a Time Three, *These are My Latest Best # 2, 3, 4, 5, 6, 7,*(All by Lulu. com)and *Growing Beyond the Fathers* (PublishAmerica, Inc).

183

THE AUTHOR'S BIO

D B. Clark is a retired Clinical Psychologist and college professor who has publish textbooks, novels, and around 90 books of poetry. with 40 years of assisting clients become more effective in living. His attempt to manage his own health is documented in his book, Dr Clark's Health Maintenance Plan.

Also, tread D.B.Clark's dally poems on donald71@allpotry.com where people from all over the would read and praise his poems.

If you have enjoyed reading this book, you might also like reading these books by D. B. Clark. Forever Young, This Garden Earth, There are My Best Poems of 2019, The Ever Returning Life of Robison Buddy Sreets (Lulu.com) Poems Promoting Painless Dying (Iuniverse.com) My Three Favorite Novels (Iuniverse.com) (Iuniverse.com)

Printed in the United States
By Bookmasters